An Afternoon to Kill

Lancelot Jones was on his way to his first job –
as tutor to an Indian Rajah's son. But the
Rajah's ancient plane and incompetent pilot
decanted him in the middle of a desert, and
the wrong desert at that. There, seeking
shade, he found, in the only dwelling of any
size within miles, a curious old Englishwoman
called Alva Hine.

Alva Hine buttonholed the prim Mr Jones
as the Ancient Mariner once made a wedding
guest his audience. She told him a strange
story of a summer fifty years ago, of love and
hate and murder in a respectable middle-class
Victorian household . . .

Julian Symons describes this masterly tour
de force, first published in 1953, as 'that
rarity, a totally original work of crime fiction.
It may enthral, amuse or annoy you,' he says,
'but you will have read nothing else quite like
it.'

SHELLEY SMITH

An Afternoon
to Kill

A Jubilee Reprint
*Selected and Introduced
by Julian Symons*

COLLINS, ST JAMES'S PLACE, LONDON

William Collins Sons & Co Ltd
London · Glasgow · Sydney · Auckland
Toronto · Johannesburg

First published 1953
Reprinted 1980
© in the Introduction, Julian Symons, 1980
Copyright reserved Shelley Smith

ISBN 0 00 231022 8

Set in Baskerville
Printed in Great Britain by
T. J. Press (Padstow) Ltd, Padstow, Cornwall
and bound by Robert Hartnoll Ltd,
Bodmin, Cornwall

For Liz
With Affection

CONTENTS

Introduction

Julian Symons

One of the pleasures in choosing the books for this Jubilee Edition has been that of enlarging my acquaintance with the work of Shelley Smith. Her best-known story is *The Ballad of the Running Man* (1961), but in a history of the crime story called *Bloody Murder* I said that her finest novel was *The Lord Have Mercy* (1956), which uses brilliantly the conventional background of middle-class English village life for most unconventional purposes. Both of these books fell outside the time scale of the Jubilee Edition, which consists of books published in the first twenty-five years of the Crime Club's life, but in any case it seems to me now that *An Afternoon to Kill* is better than either of them. This masterly tour de force is that rarity, a totally original work of crime fiction. It may enthral, amuse or annoy you, but you will have read nothing else quite like it.

The surprising thing about Shelley Smith's crime stories is indeed their variety. She has explored particularly that grey area in which petty villainy may move on to murder. Her protagonists often have no particular wish to kill, but are simply so callous that they do so when need arises without any of those moral twinges that affect most of us even in relation to minor wrongdoing. Thomas Bates in *Man Alone* is led to a grotesque impersonation and to violence by a passion for luxury combined with extreme avarice. *The Woman in the Sea* is based fairly closely on the real life murder case of Alma Rattenbury, and adds some interesting and plausible psychological speculation to the known facts. *This is the House,* a more orthodox but still unusual kind of crime story, gives us two murders set on a West Indian island, and a most ingenious plot. In *Come and Be Killed* dullish neurotic Florence runs away from the nursing home to which she has been consigned by her busy sister, and meets kindly Mrs Jolly. But kindly women in these books are rarely what they seem. Mrs Jolly is a murderess, although one (a nice touch this) too tender-hearted actually to watch her victim die.

Writers determined to be original take considerable risks. When their characterisation fails to convince they let down the reader with a thump, and not all of Shelley Smith's books are successes. But among those I have mentioned, *Come and Be Killed* and *The Woman in the Sea* emphatically deserve a place on the shelves of every crime addict whose taste ranges outside the pure puzzle. It is deplorable that both, and indeed so much of Shelley Smith's other work, should be out of print.

An Afternoon to Kill has almost from the opening pages the shimmering quality of a mirage. Young Lancelot Jones is being flown out to his first job, that of tutor to an Indian Rajah's son, and the incompetent pilot lands him in a desert. Something is wrong with the plane, but what? Are they on the Iranian Plateau, as the pilot says, or somewhere else altogether? Does the distant building that quivers in the heat 'like a pearly blemish where the japanned sky met the earth' really exist? It has a physical presence, yet we have an impression of unreality, even though the person who greets Lancelot is solid enough, 'a sturdy wide-hipped old woman like a peasant, with her white hair cropped as short as a man's'. Her name is Alva Hine, which means nothing to Lancelot, a severe young man who prefers facts to fantasies and regards novels as 'a pernicious infection of the mind'. The old woman is annoyed by his priggishness, and starts to tell him a story . . .

The atmosphere of *The Thousand and One Nights* is invoked quite deliberately, and maintained throughout the story. While the plane is being repaired Lancelot sits spellbound, listening to Alva's life story, a dramatic tale of Victorian mystery and melodrama. He makes occasional interjections, and in the end comes to a conclusion that we may already have reached. Yet a deception is involved. When we look back on the tale after reading the last page, and refer again to the opening chapter, we appreciate fully the fine cunning with which we have been tricked.

That is all it is proper to say about the book, and I know little of the author. Shelley Smith is a pseudonym used by Nancy Hermione Bodington. She once studied painting, spent a brief married life in an Italian castle, and now lives in Sussex. She is one of the crime story's artists, not one of its journeymen.

PROLOGUE

THE HOUSE IN THE DESERT

It was the hour before high noon when the old-fashioned aeroplane that was taking the English tutor from England to the remote little Indian state came out of the vast empty sky and quavered down upon the sun-bleached silent land. The pilot clambered down and slowly walked round the machine; but as soon as the Englishman called out to know what was wrong he changed the expression of anxiety on his brown face to a grin of cheerful confidence.

'Is all right. I fix,' he said, with an airy wave of the hand, as if he knew what was wrong.

The Englishman climbed down to join him.

'What's the damage?' he said again.

'Bust the under carriage on these damn stones you see,' the pilot said, kicking it. 'Not too bad. Might be worse. And a little engine trouble. Is nothing. I soon fix.'

'Where are we?'

The pilot would like to have known this too; for he had no idea how far off-course he was. He also did not know what was wrong with the machine, or how long it would take him to mend it. He was badly frightened under his nervous veneer of competence. If something went wrong and the Englishman – well, if the Englishman never arrived, then he, Ras Ali, would be finished, ruined, disgraced (it had not yet occurred to him that if the Englishman did not arrive presumably neither would he); he saw his thin dark little wife and the children with their poor little hands raised tremblingly for mercy, and he wanted to weep. The baked yellowish earth patched with brown grass and stunted thorn bushes (a landscape like the end of the world) began to shimmer in his tear-filled eyes.

'We are in the desert,' he said. But then this tiresome Englishman with his passion for facts demanded to know which desert.

'Perhaps the Iranian Plateau.'

'What do you mean, "perhaps the Iranian Plateau"? Don't you *know* where we are?'

'Well, it is the Iranian Plateau,' said Ras Ali, convinced by his own words.

The Englishman frowned.

'We shouldn't be anywhere near Iran, surely?'

'Oh, another route,' said the little man, again with an airy gesture of the hand. 'Just as good. Quicker. Better,' he improvised.

The Englishman was just about to explode into rage at this stupid lie when he thought it would be seemlier to appear cool and amused by the situation. At Oxford one was expected to remain the cool spectator in all circumstances. In *all* circumstances. And Mr Jones was profoundly serious about this philosophically detached attitude to life. (Mr Jones was twenty-four.) So he smiled down at the absurd little man and said:

'It's damned hot out here, I think I'll get back into the plane while you get on with the job. I'm afraid I'm no use with machinery at all.'

But the plane was unbearably hot and stuffy inside, the sun's rays seemed all to converge on this metal box, charging it with heat. And Mr Jones very soon stumbled out gasping like a landed flounder. He thought to seat himself in the shade of the machine. But the sun was already too high. The narrow black places were intolerable.

He shielded his glasses and peered short-sightedly at the bare horizon quivering in the heat surrounding them. Through the distorting glare of heat there did seem to be something. A mark like a pearly blemish where the japanned sky met the earth. He called Ras Ali. It was a building, the pilot declared after an instant's scrutiny. And from a building help might be forthcoming, he realised

jubilantly, and at once offered to go and see. But Mr Jones
firmly nipped that suggestion; the pilot should stay with his
plane and get on with the job of mending it. If there was any
form of help coming from this building Mr Jones would
send it.

'You will not leave me alone in this desert all night!' cried
the pilot.

'All *night*! How long is it going to take you to do this job?'
said Mr Jones in equal dismay.

'Two days, three days, I cannot tell, I do not know,' wept
the little man.

'Nonsense,' said Mr Jones languidly, savouring his own
aplomb. 'It can't possibly be anything serious. Dirty plugs,
I expect. We've got to get going, you know, we can't be
stranded out here.'

'No, sir. Jolly well right you are. I fix it at once, right
away, this afternoon. I will be ten minutes,' he promised,
recalling the notices he had seen pinned to obscure English
shops: 'Back in ten minutes.'

But Mr Jones was taking no chances. Besides, even
standing in this fierce heat made him feel dizzy. 'It must be
finished this afternoon,' he said, tucking a handkerchief
under his topee to protect the back of his neck, and then he
walked away towards what he sincerely hoped was not a
mirage. He dwindled from the pilot's sight . . .

He approached a high wall with dark windows cut in it
here and there like dominoes. He walked round two sides of
the wall before he found the way in; a small gate black as
iron. He rang and turned, waiting, to see in the distance the
piled white boxes of a village and the beautiful liquid mirror
of a lake or reservoir. When he returned impatiently to the
gate he wondered how long those eyes had been watching
him through the grille.

It couldn't have been harder to get inside if it had been a
harem, and not for want of comprehension, for the doorkeeper spoke an adequate sort of basic English.

'Take me to your master,' demanded Jones impatiently,

tired of this oriental beating about the bush.

The cross-eyed doorkeeper looked at his left ear and the ghost standing at his right-hand side at the same instant, and said with all the decision of an English butler:

'She not possible see anyone.'

Mr Jones thought, 'I shall expire if I don't get out of this heat,' and desperation spurred his addled wits into commonsense. He brought out a handful of money. The bolts slid cautiously back.

The courtyard was like Paradise. There was shade and scent, and that sound as refreshing as a breeze, the lucid tinkle of water. A jasmine cast a filigree of shade on one side to the edge of an inner colonnade. A china rose offered its hundred blossoms to the sun. But Mr Jones was not permitted to linger within the discreet gaze of those latticed windows. He was urged towards an inner apartment, large and dim with a bizarred design of sunlight on the floor. He looked about him, blinking, dazzled by the sudden duskiness. He presumed the servant had scuffed off to fetch someone; but whom? 'She not possible see anyone,' he remembered, and imagined a wealthy Moslem widow in 'purdah'. On the mother-of-pearl table beneath the pierced lattice a cricket chirped perpetually in its little paper cage. The sound was insistent, hypnotic, and he stared at the little creature absorbedly.

He was quite ridiculously startled when a voice suddenly bade him, 'Good afternoon!' He swung round in quite a tiz. He thought at first it was a man standing in the archway. Then he saw it was an old woman, a sturdy wide-hipped old woman like a peasant, with her white hair cropped as short as a man's. She came forward.

'I'm sorry I startled you,' she said in a deep pleasant voice.

'You're English!' he exclaimed, for some reason astonished beyond words at finding an English woman in this oriental citadel.

'And so are you, and I could not resist hearing the tones

of an English voice again after all these years.'

'It's extraordinary,' he murmured.

'You are easily astonished,' she said with a faint smile. 'I shall introduce myself. I am Alva Hine.' She saw the name meant nothing to him.

'My name is Lancelot Jones,' he said, 'and I'm supposed to be flying out to Bandrapore, as tutor to Mahmoud Kahn's son. But we were forced to come down here with engine trouble, and I've left the pilot to tinker up the machine while I came out to see if there was any help to be got. I don't know anything about machinery myself, but it strikes me that the pilot is a complete fool, and I believe he's just been flying blind,' he said, at last acknowledging to himself his ludicrous plight.

The old woman said:

'Then you didn't come to see me?'

'Dear me,' said Lancelot Jones, who had vaguely supposed her position in this household equivalent to what his own was to be in Bandrapore. 'Actually, no.' He looked attentively now at that square majestic head which bore in its features the nobility of some ancient granite sculpture. 'I suppose then you are She?' he tentatively suggested.

'She?'

He explained the 'She not possible see anyone'.

'Oh! Like Ayesha,' she chuckled.

'I beg your pardon?'

'Ayesha,' she repeated, 'the wonderful white goddess. Rider Haggard. Don't you remember?'

'A book?' he hazarded.

'I have put the fear of God into them of course. I had to. They know I never see anyone.'

'You've been out here a long time.'

'Many years,' she said, 'many years. But you, I am sure, are not anxious to stay as long as that. They will be expecting you in Bandrapore. How long were you thinking of staying here? There is nothing in the vicinity to attract a stranger, I'm afraid, and I fear you'll find my poor hospi-

tality very primitive,' she announced with placid cruelty.
'Dear lady, I hope I shall not have to stay at all,' he said
hastily. 'If you could shelter me for just a few hours, I think
the pilot will have put it in order.'

'I shall send my chauffeur to help him, he is quite clever
with engines, I find.' She clapped her hands and gave an
order to a servant. 'Now tell me all about yourself, Mr
Jones?' she commanded as imperiously as a child awaiting a
fairy story.

But either there was nothing to tell, or he did not know
how to tell it. He told her he was twenty-four . . . His
father . . . His mother . . . Oxford . . . Alva Hine patted
away a little yawn. This was not worth while disturbing
herself for, she thought, studying the serious young man
with his long thin legs poking up in front of him. If she was
disappointed it did not show in her serene face.

A servant brought in little glasses of sweet mint tea.

'Tell me about London,' she said. 'What goes on there,
and who are the novelists you admire to-day?' she said,
searching for a suitable subject of conversation for this dull
young man.

'I never read novels.'

'My dear young man!' she expostulated with some irritation. 'Why not, may I ask?'

'You may indeed. They don't interest me.'

'But why not?' she insisted.

'Frankly, I can't see the point,' he shrugged. 'Even if I
had the time to waste (which I haven't) I don't believe I
should ever come to reading novels. I really cannot fathom
why anyone ever does.'

'Or write them, I suppose.'

'No, I can't say that. There are such an immense number
of curious ways of earning a living, that I suppose writing
fiction is no odder than any other. But why anyone should
bother to read it is another matter. A pernicious infection of
the mind.'

'You think so?'

'At any time. But at this period of history when one really does feel that one cannot be too serious in one's approach to the problems of this age, why fritter one's valuable energies away on such senseless frivolity which weakens the moral fibre – so my tutor always said – and dulls the intellect,' said Lancelot Jones in wise lecture-room tones, approving the sonorous periods.

The old woman smiled at the ridiculous young prig.

'You have nothing to learn,' she said.

'No, but you do see what I mean?'

'Ah, I see; but I like to wander through these childhood groves of fantasy you so disapprove of. It seems to me that I am looking at my own heart in a mirror, and seeing there things I never knew I knew.'

'What sort of things?' he said like a chess-player.

'Secrets about the nature of humanity.'

'Then why not study psychology, my dear madam, which would unfold to you the meaning of these secrets you find so esoteric?' He made a very slight gesture with one tense hand, which betrayed his excitement.

'Have you ever considered,' she said slowly and now quite seriously too, 'that there are truths that are not strictly communicable in words, or are conveyed somehow beyond the total effect of the book? Like the ungraspable truths of lyric poetry. But I suppose that poetry, too, is beneath your consideration.'

'I want *facts,* not poetry,' he cried. 'Poetry was good enough for me when I was jogged up and down on my mother's knee before I could speak. Poetry is for the infancy of the world, or the slack irresponsible dreamer, or the dictator who uses words to hypnotise people. Down with poetry, I say; it has been a curse to mankind!'

' "Milton, thou should'st be living at this hour!" ' she remarked. 'I can see that if I am to be allowed to retain my own feeble convictions of what constitutes noble pleasure – let us call it "the right to the pursuit of happiness" – we must find some other subject for discussion. You shall choose this time, it is your turn.'

He hesitated.

'May it be personal? May I ask why you live in this strange solitary place?'

She was silent, thinking. Her round brown hands lay quietly in her lap.

'I will tell you,' she said at the end of her deliberations. 'It is all so long ago now it cannot matter. I should like to tell it to someone, and it will help to kill the hours of waiting for you, perhaps. I shall try not to bore you,' she added considerately.

CHAPTER ONE

THE HOUSE BY THE SEA

The old woman began dreamily:

'It is like pulling back veil after veil from the past to find the beginning of the story that ended with my coming here. And now that I examine it, I can think of no other place to begin than the beginning – when we were all children and lived in a massive pink and yellow crenellated Victorian house with a clock-tower. It stood out hideously in that bleak Essex landscape; but its shrubberies and all those deadly dark evergreens made it a romantic place for children to play and hide and dream in, swaying high up in the shadowy branches of a cedar. And the rambling echoey house too was just what children like. I suppose that was why Father bought it. It was so suitable for a large and growing family. And there was a railway in the village not far away to take Father to Town. Father was a tea merchant. Once a year we children were taken on a pilgrimage to the warehouses in Stepney and the business in the City, queer-smelling dusty old places with flights of stairs that made my young legs ache.

'It must have been quite a prosperous business, since it supported our large family in comfort, though we lived plainly and sensibly with our nurses and governesses, very much in awe of our parents, at least of Papa. He was a tall man with a stern pale face and dark eyes. His whiskers and eyebrows were handsomely black in my recollection of him, although his hair was already crowded with silver. I thought he was God,' the old woman said with a simple smile.

'I loved Mama. That was different. But Papa I adored. I think the boys were frightened of him. His displeasure could be terrible. I wasn't afraid of him. I only wanted to be his favourite, and when poor little Ursula died I became the eldest girl – "Papa's pet". There were – let me see – eight of us in all, counting the ones who didn't live to grow up. There was Percival, who was nine years older than me, and Ursula who died when she was thirteen, and Mary who died as a baby, and Robert, and then me, Blanche Rose – Oh,' she said, catching the young man's surprised look, 'Alva Hine is only the name I am known by now, it's not my real name. Blanche Rose was my parents' cruel choice for a girl who turned out to be about as unlike a white rose as a girl can. Poor lanky, graceless, shy Blanche Rose! And after her came Harry, as handsome and cheerful as Blanche was plain and awkward. And then Lucy, a pretty little fair child like Mama.

'It must have been a bitter blow for Papa when Percival elected to go into the Indian Army instead of the business. The eldest boy and all that, you know. And then Robert was a disappointment too. He did something disgraceful and ran away, and we children were never allowed to utter his name again. But I was still a child at that time, and I did not understand or care. My elder brothers were so far above me that I hardly missed them anyway. My own life was absorbedly busy then. Until I was fourteen I imagined that life was meant to be enjoyed.

'But when I was fourteen Mama died. They can never have meant to have another child after Lucy, and when Edgar was born it killed her. Not at once. For some weeks she seemed uncertain whether she wanted to live or die, and I remember how impressed and terrified I was by the sense of illness in the house, the hush, the solemn crackling nurse, and the breath-catching odour of disinfectants, and Mama looking horribly small and yellow suddenly in the big white bed. And then one day, I don't know why, I suddenly realised that she was going to die, that death was inescapable. I couldn't bear to see her after that. But when she lay dying with all her children around her and Papa kneeling at her side with his face in his hands (Weeping? Or praying?), she took my cold hand weakly in her burning one and whispered, "Look after Papa, my little girl." And I promised with all the passion of my young heart.

'I meant to be very grown-up and good and useful to him. I would have done anything to please him, I loved him so. And in fact I did entirely take my cue from him. At that most impressionable age I saw life altogether through his eyes. I wanted to be like him, austere and noble and melancholy; I wished I too had black hair and eyes instead of my long straight dull brown hair and ordinary grey eyes. *He possessed my imagination.*

'In some mysterious way the house seemed to go to pieces without anything being changed when Mama died. It was always cheerless and cold now. The trees grew too near the house and made it dark. There was an air of crape about the silent unvisited rooms where we children were seldom to be seen (except that as the eldest child at home I took my place at the vast mahogany dinner-table in the sombre green dining-room with its stolid pheasants and fish in their gilt frames, and tried to entertain Papa with the polite trivialities I had heard Mama dispense). It was as though the soul had left the house. I thought that must be the way Papa wanted it. One had always an impression of dust on the furniture, though I suppose it was clean enough really. Yet I understood emotionally that Papa was *mourning.* I had a queer childish exaggerated idea of love and I was afraid that he would not want to live without her. And it may indeed have been only his duty to his children that kept him wearily working. And yet he hardly seemed aware of us. Every morning we came to give him an obedient kiss as he sat at his solitary breakfast with the paper unopened beside him. Lucy fetched his umbrella; I his top-hat; and then, with our noses pressed into green triangles on the window, we watched the carriage clatter away into the grey sea-mist. Then Lucy in her black pinafore scampered up to her governess and I more slowly followed in the weight of my

heavy mourning – somehow one could not run in black, one
felt too responsible, too grown-up, too consciously sad. And
all day long I nervously waited for the evening when, with
hair neatly brushed back and fastened with a black ribbon
and a locket round my neck, I went down to dinner and
tried to engage Papa in conversation. I never succeeded in
making him smile, I doubt if he even heard my awkward
efforts. It was misery to me. Because I loved him this was
the high spot of my day, and I always believed that I failed
him. Till I hit on the idea of reading the paper aloud to him
as he ate; a solution which absolved us both.

'Every Sunday we took flowers to the churchyard; but
Papa never spoke to us about Mama, and I used to pretend
that the flowers on the grave had nothing to do with her. I
think I must have been very lonely at this time. It was an
unnatural life. We visited nobody and no children ever
came to play with us. We might have been living a hundred
miles from any other habitation instead of a quarter of an
hour's walk from the huddled little village. Yet I had grown
to like the life. I wanted Papa to remain for ever with me in
this dark unreal world of the past. I wanted to take Mama's
place with Papa.'

Lancelot Jones sat up more alertly, and behind his
glasses he raised his eyebrows.

'That shocks you,' siad the old woman, smiling faintly.

'Oh, not at all,' Lancelot Jones hastened to assure her.
'I'm not *shocked.* We all know about the Oedipus complex
now. The only thing about it that *is* horrifying to our
twentieth-century minds is that the Victorians in their
innocence found the perverse sexual relationship between
parent and child "pretty", something to be encouraged and
fostered. I confess that does make me feel rather ill. It apparently never occurred to them that it was not only
dangerous but often disastrous for the child.'

'Not for Miss Mitford, not for Elizabeth Barrett
Browning, not – if I dare put myself among such august
company – for me,' said the sturdy old woman equably.

'I don't think you *quite* understand,' said Lancelot Jones
kindly.

'But I do,' she said cheerfully. 'You think I do not realise
that I was in love with my own father; yet that is exactly
what I have been at some pains to describe to you, my dear
young man, in the simplest language possible, so that you
could not fail to understand. It was a tragedy, and from it
came tragedy. There is no need to veil one's meaning
behind the timeless antics of Greek mythology.'

He arched his brows politely.

'Yet you say that it was not disastrous for you.'

'Look at me!' she said, sitting there with her hands on her
knees like a fat brown goddess, placid and ironical. 'Am I
not what they call "an integrated personality"?'

He gazed at her in silence.

'Well?' she said.

'I do not pretend to be a psychologist,' he said modestly
at last. 'But, if you will allow me to say so, even I can see
signs of a deep-seated neurosis in your retreat from life.'

'You interest me strangely,' she smiled. 'What makes you
think so?'

'Your living here, cut off from the world and your own
kind of people.'

'But I have not yet told you why I came here.'

'True, but there *is* a reason for it, there is a story behind
your coming here, a story whose origins lie far back in your
life. "It is all such a long time ago," you said when I asked
you. You did not say, "I came because the climate suited
me," or "I had work to do here," or in fact anything rational
that could be explained in a sentence.'

'In a sentence, I came because I wanted to get as far away
as possible from England to some corner of the world so
remote that my name would be unknown and no one would
have heard of me. Does that do?'

'Yet you see you didn't get away at all. You uncon-
sciously sought out a place that bore for you all the salient
characteristics of "home".'

'Now how do you make that out?' she said, astonished.

'It's really rather interesting; the pattern is quite blatant. You come to a country where the thought is predominantly Mahommedan and the women are kept in submission, just as you must have been when you were young in Victorian England; you choose a place where the empty stretch of tawny earth and the enormous arch of unobstructed sky is in some odd way not at all unlike the Essex coast; you create about you the atmosphere of your "dark home" (where the trees grew too near the house with its gloomy Victorian draperies) even here, where the sun is so strong that it has to be filtered through pierced gratings; you have even set yourself a little away from the village so that you can live in studied isolation, "visiting no one, and with no one coming to see you".'

The old woman with her strong mannish head and cropped white hair began to laugh, began to shake with silent and prolonged laughter.

'But you are – you really are – extraordinarily clever, my dear young sir – a quite brilliant piece of induction,' she gasped. 'I had no idea – very remarkable how it all fits – you have declared me to myself.' She passed a hand across her mouth as though to wipe away her mirth, and said more seriously: 'But why is that "disastrous", if I am happy here, after all?'

'Because – don't you see? – you can only be happy *here,* where you can live your fantasy-life undisturbed, where you need never grow up and face life's realities. You never have escaped from your childhood, you have simply hidden yourself inescapably in the past. Even when you thought you had broken away you came to live in a place that reminded you of the past, you were always in your heart trying to "get back", you see.'

'My dear, it sounds *frantically* Barrie-ish,' old Miss Hine murmured. 'Blanche Rose is one thing, but the idea of "Mary Rose" is somehow infinitely depressing. That was not what I was trying to convey at all.'

'I beg your pardon?' he said with a puzzled air.

'Ah, I fancy that's a myth you will not have heard of,' she said demurely. 'A myth, the meaning of which I suppose you could say was, that it is always too late, really from the moment one is born.'

'Oh, I don't say that. That is a hopelessly futile and defeatist attitude. One must be practical. One must learn to adjust oneself to an adult conception of life.'

'At my age that would be rather difficult, I suppose,' old Miss Hine said meekly.

A servant speaking from the archway made him jump, and spared him the embarrassment of replying, he didn't want to hurt the old lady's feelings.

Alva Hine rose and led the way into a beautiful room with a domed ceiling and blue walls with a design of Arabic script in white lettering running along the top. The windows in here were unlatticed, narrow apertures with a thin column dividing each one into two with a rather pretty and graceful effect. An exquisite carpet hung on one wall, the only ornament. And there was no furniture to fuss the eye as in a European room, except for a table eighteen inches high with a big beaten silver dish on it piled with melons, figs, ruddy peaches, and small black grapes.

Imitating her example, he folded himself as awkwardly as a camel on to his cushion, while the servant held before him a great platter of meats dyed saffron on a bed of rice garnished with stewed guavas and black olives, from which arose the mingled scents of oil and garlic and spices. Lancelot Jones became suddenly aware that he was exceedingly hungry.

'This is amazingly good,' he said, the juices running down his chin as he munched.

'Just boiled mutton and rice like we used to have at home when I was a girl,' she added blandly. 'I expect that's why I like it,' she added, her innocent eye on his.

He had the grace to smile.

'I see you have a sense of humour.'

'That at least was something I've acquired that I hadn't when I was young. As Cousin Nell used to say to me reprovingly twenty times a day, "Laugh, and the world laughs with you," and "A merry heart goes all the way"; she was a great one for tags. Not that she was particularly merry herself, poor old soul, but she wasn't used to children and this seemed to her a happy way of correcting their little faults without nagging. I think we would all rather have been ill-treated even. We despised Cousin Nell. She was a tiresome old bore and we thought her slightly ridiculous, in the intolerant way children have of judging their elders. She was a cousin of Mother's, and when Mother died she came down from Scotland to look after us all. She cannot have been happy with us, all her efforts were quite unappreciated. And though we were never actively rude or played practical jokes on her, we ignored her, which was worse. I often wonder she stayed so dauntlessly. I suppose it was her sense of duty. She actually cried when she left. But then,' she added thoughtfully, 'so did we.

'She was a hopeless spinster of course, and must have been nearly as old as Father – quite fifty, I imagine, yet I fancy she had her dreams, her mad wild hopes and fears, poor sentimental old horse with her ear-rings tinkling like a bridle. She never was silly with Father, she behaved with scrupulous decency always, but if she had not been a little in love with Father herself, would there have been all those jealous scenes between us?

'We disagreed profoundly in our interpretation of Papa's wishes, and these disagreements always ended in the same way, with me storming from the house in a passion to walk broodingly for hours by the restless sea, or across the fields of harsh grey stubble where the stunted trees seemed to be clinging to the earth by their heels, like gnarled old country-women with their skirts blown over their heads by the cutting salt wind.

'Night would fall and owls begin to hoot and I would huddle among the dunes watching the lights go up in the houses in the village, waiting for the sound of Papa's carriage returning from the station. Then I would gather my heavy skirts with their sodden sand-encrusted hem into my two hands and spring in beside him as he passed. He would look at me, at my wind-tangled hair and white exhausted face, with his solemn black eyes and say nothing. But I would never know what he was thinking, and in a sudden access of guilt would feel wretchedly uncertain of my case, and I would cry out: "Papa, I've been wicked!" and follow it immediately with the accusation: "Cousin Nell is a beast! I hate her!" Papa would look at me in pained silence till I began to cry and then he would catch me into his arms and stroke my hair and murmur sadly, "My poor little motherless girl!" Ah, those were really the moments of my life! When I felt close to him and my heart seemed ready to burst with a deliciously painful joy. Once I murmured, "I wish we need never go back," but Papa's only thought was to reach the sad comfort of his home, the solace of a fire and a glass of sherry and the evening paper in unbroken peace, after his long day in the City. I would stalk proudly into the house on his arm, looking like a scarecrow no doubt, but feeling like a black-clad Infanta of Spain. I would eye Cousin Nell defiantly where she sat nursing her dignity with her sewing beneath the gaslight that turned her sandy-grey hair to a livid gamboge. But the next day I would be very, very polite and obedient to Cousin Nell, who, as like as not, would merely say, "'Tis never too late to mend," or "Vengeance is mine, saith the Lord; I will repay," delivered with an absent air as though these cryptic laconisms had nothing to do with whatever we were talking about.'

She took a slice of melon steeped in stem ginger, and added:

'So we dwelt, and continued to dwell, in this curious limbo of the defunct for four years.'

CHAPTER TWO

A CARRIAGE IN THE RAIN

'Yes, four years,' she went on mediatively, wiping her fingers. 'I was nearly eighteen, when the first, the very first breath of change ruffled the calm of our strange life. I remember it well, that June day. A day of chill ceaseless rain with the sea a pallid dishwater colour beneath the leaden sky. It was too wet to go out, and Edgar cooped up in his nursery all day had been as naughty as an indefatigable four-year-old can be. He threw Lucy's exercise-books out of the window on to the muddy path beneath and then screamed when Lucy slapped him. He would not play, he would not do his lessons, he would not sit quietly and listen to a story. "He was a bad, disobedient, unruly boy, and Papa would have to be told." "Damn!" said Edgar with a wicked look in his eye. "Oh, that's too much, you naughty boy; you shall be sent to bed!" he was told. "Damn! Damn! Damn! Damn! Damn! Damn! Damn!" said Edgar, cheerfully of the opinion that one might as well be hung for a sheep as a lamb. Now Papa would certainly have to be told, and Papa would be very very angry.

'But Papa was late that night; a thing that never happened, he was as punctual as Immanuel Kant. And in such rain too! Could there have been an accident, the carriage overturned, the horse bolted, we were beginning anxiously to wonder, when Papa's key jingled in the door. He came in whistling faintly through pursed lips and rattling his keys jauntily in his pocket.

'We were surprised – and something more, some uneasiness, or dismay, entered my heart at least. But we all ran to him like well-trained loving hens:

' "Papa!" we cried. "What happened to you? You're so *late!*" we cried.

'He looked at his watch solemnly and said he was exactly thirty-eight minutes late, but there was a hint of a smile in his voice.

' "Were my chicks worried about their poor old father? Did they fear they had lost their breadwinner? And may he be allowed to refresh himself somewhat, take off his wet boots, and warm himself by the fire, before he embarks on the narrative of his adventures?"

'We cosseted him and patted him and sat him by the fire with his glass of Madeira, and Lucy knelt at his feet and I leaned against his chair with my arm on his shoulders, and Cousin Nell picked up her sewing again with Harry cross-legged on the mat beside her.

'I can see it as clearly as a picture in the family album; a little tableau of a happy family; and it may be because it was fundamentally the last evening like that, with Papa still in our possession, that the recollection of that moment is still so vivid to me.

'And then father began to tell us his pathetically respectable little adventure, how he descended from the train to find a damsel in distress cowering from the rain in her pretty summer frock, trying to keep her wide-brimmed hat from blowing away with one hand, and her skirts from the puddles with the other. And Father had offered her his carriage to her destination, which after some little persuasion she had accepted. He had then to wait in the cold draughty station himself for the carriage to return.

' "But why didn't you go with her, Papa?" Lucy cried.

' "That would not have been proper, my child," said Papa mildly.

' "Well, I don't call that much of an adventure!" pouted Lucy. "Do you, Harry?"

'But Papa only smiled and pulled her curls, and said he was too old for proper adventures now. "And what does my big girl say?" he asked, turning to me.

'I took a sip of Madeira from his glass and said: "Who was she, Papa?"

' "I've no idea," said Papa. "I have never seen her before. I should not have forgotten if I had."

' "Goodness, how mysterious," I said, "perhaps she had escaped from an asylum, like The Woman in White."

' "She was in white," Papa said, "a white frock with black velvet bands on it and a white straw hat with black velvet ribbons."

'Papa to say this, who never noticed what anyone wore! I felt a strange sensation in my breast and I laughed and said, "She must have looked ridiculous in all that rain!"

'And then we changed the subject and talked of other things till Papa's dinner was ready.

'The event would have passed from my mind if Papa had not received two days later a letter in a pretty florid hand thanking him for his kindness, and passed it across to me, saying, "My fair unknown!"

'It was signed Sophia Falk with a broad flourish such as a queen might give to her signature. For some reason that signature made me fear the writer's personality. I could think of nothing to say but, "She's staying with Mrs Livingstone." Mrs Livingstone we knew, she was a respectable but indigent gentlewoman who lived in a seedy unattractive house at the wrong end of the High Street, near the gasworks. Mama did not exactly call on her, but I knew she was considered a useful person to help with Bazaars and Flag Days. She was now evidently reduced to taking in "summer visitors" as lodgers were euphemistically called in those days.

'I thought in the circumstances it was rather "fast" of this Miss Falk to have written to Papa when she had not been introduced to him.

' "Perhaps," said Papa vaguely, thinking of other things.

'On Sunday as we came out of church into the sunshine, little Mrs Livingstone came hurrying up to Papa, putting her gloved hands together as if in prayer, and said:

' "Oh, Mr Sheridan, I really *must* be allowed to thank you for your very great kindness to my niece the other evening. Such consideration!"
' "Ah, your niece!" said Papa.
' "Yes. Sophia dear, come here! Such a *dear* girl! So *artistic*!" confided Mrs Livingstone; but I was watching Miss Falk come with modestly downcast eyes past the throng at the porch with a swift graceful walk, in the cream-coloured tussore with the black bands and the demurest little velvet bonnet imaginable, beneath which were folded two wings of smooth red hair. She carried aloft a white lace parasol, like a trim little sail. She did not raise her eyes to Papa's when Mrs Livingstone introduced her but put out a small kid-clad hand and said with a tiny smile: "We meet again," in a way that made me feel she was inviting Papa to laugh with her at her aunt, who all this while was still uttering a stream of banalities.

'I thought she was astonishingly beautiful, and I could not imagine why I did not like her or why she made me feel afraid.

'Papa said, "These are my children: Blanche Rose, Lucy, Harry. You must come and take tea with them one day, if you will; they are dull. My sister-in-law will write and arrange a convenient day."

'Miss Falk made no reply because she was looking at me, or rather at my clothes and hair, so that I became instantly flamingly aware of my dowdy black dress and the absurd straw hat with marguerites that was so much too childish for my serious young face, I was conscious of my awkward long limbs, that I had not yet learned to use with grace, and the frayed tip of my black cotton glove where I chewed it habitually during the sermon, and the dust on my shoes because I still scuffed them like a child as I walked. I felt intolerably foolish and ugly under Miss Falk's cool gaze that did not trouble to meet mine but passed on to Lucy and, meeting her smile of candid admiration, responded with the beginnings of a smile whose full flower was only received by Harry. Whereas I was clumsy and long-limbed as a boy, Harry was a pretty schoolboy with a girl's delicate complexion and Father's black curling hair. For just a moment Miss Falk looked full into Harry's eyes and her smile was tender and understanding and a little amused. Harry blushed till his ears were red as roses. Poor Harry! He was hers from that moment.

' "Whew! Isn't she a stunner?" he breathed to me as we walked away.

'I didn't answer. I didn't want to have her to tea, but I was careful not to say so, hoping that if nothing was said, Papa might forget about it. I could not imagine what had made Papa ask her; no one had been to tea since Mama died. It was a strange impulse of his, that with luck would pass away. But he mentioned it at Sunday dinner to Cousin Nell, and a week later Miss Falk came to tea.

'She wore a dove-grey silk, I remember, and a green bonnet with a feather. I coveted that bonnet though I knew I should have looked absurd in it. She did not speak much, but looked around her under her eyelids, appraisingly. I walked her about the grounds. She said she thought the house charmingly pretty.

' "We don't think so," I said scornfully.

'She assured me she was quite a judge of houses, and added with a little modest air, hanging her head: "I paint houses, you see."

'I burst out laughing involuntarily, so unused was I to the niceties of social intercourse. Faint rose stained her ivory cheek. She bit her lip. I apologised through my mirth. "It sounded as if . . . " I attempted to explain stupidly.

' "It pleases you to make fun of me," she said, with such sharpness that it almost brought tears to my eyes.

' "I didn't mean . . . " I began with a look of horror, but she took no notice and went on icily:

' "How should you know what it means to be obliged to earn your own living with something so fragile as a pencil and a box of colours? Because you have a father, does that

give you the right to sneer at me, as though I was not as
respectable and well-bred as yourself?"

' "I didn't, I didn't," I stammered, that quiet voice
turning like a blade in my breast. We were sauntering so
gently across the lawn that no one would have guessed the
rage and mortification that consumed us.

' "Do you suppose because one has the misfortune to be
poor, one's feelings are *less* sensitive than people's whose
pride is banked about with money?" she ground out bitterly, in a tone that left me in no doubt as to *her* feelings.

'I could not understand why my stupid remark should
have made her so angry with me.'

'Resentment,' murmured Lancelot Jones, cracking a
peach-stone with his teeth.

'Oh, of course. But then, you see . . . I was so appallingly
ignorant. Girls were, you know. Moreover, I was frightened
by her. People had been cross with me often enough, sometimes unjustly, but no one had ever, really never, spoken to
me with hatred before. It made my knees shake. It made me
want to bolt indoors and hide myself in the attic among the
trunks and broken chairs and Mama's clothes.'

'It didn't make you want to hit back?'

'Oh, no. It made me feel ashamed.'

'So already, you see, there was this reluctance in you to
face life and come to terms with it. Your impulse was to
retreat, back, back to the womb, to undisturbed privacy
and the aroma of Mama,' he delineated pleasurably.

'All the same, I didn't go,' she reminded him. 'I walked
miserably beside her listening to the bitter contempt in her
voice, as though it was my fault that she had taken a
pleurisy executing a commission in the spring, which had
obliged her to waste the height of her "season" recuperating
down here at her aunt's. We were walking through the
shrubbery at the time and I pulled at the leaves as I passed
and crushed them in my fingers. The scent of bay brings
back that feeling of puzzled guilt even now.

'That evening when Papa asked how the tea-party had

gone, I found myself asking him if he wouldn't commission
Miss Falk to do a water-colour of The Grange.

' "She's dreadfully poor," I murmured, fingering his
watch chain, "and she's been ill besides." He seemed
pleased with me for suggesting it. I suppose he was glad of
the excuse.

'So he arranged it. And presently from the front windows
could be seen her little figure in a fawn dust-coat sitting very
upright on her stool every fine afternoon, glancing up at the
house and marking what she saw on to the block on her
knee.

' "You mustn't bother her," I said, but the children
would run down directly lessons were over; and from the
schoolroom window I saw her laughing with them.

'Harry's great hobby was photography, and he spent
hours with his apparatus fussing about to get a picture at
exactly the angle from which she was working, to help her
with the drawing and perspective. And then hours more in
his dark-room fiddling about with "washes" and trying to
enlarge the print to the same size as her painting. Sometimes I wished I had never been so stupid as to suggest the
work in the first place. Often she would still be there
industriously "at it" in the late afternoon when Papa
returned. And he would have his Madeira brought out to
him on the lawn and a glass for her as well. He must have
thought he was merely being courteous to a gallant young
woman, asking kindly questions which she lobbed back to
him in all discretion. What amazed me was to hear him
laughing. I could not ever remember having heard him
laugh before, and the sound chilled me to a standstill. There
is this little picture frozen in my memory of him sitting on
the grass at her feet laughing up at her like a boy with a look
of astonishment at himself in his eyes; and she with bent
head trailing her brush along the bottom of the paper, so
that I could not see the expression on her face.

'I was jealous and afraid of her and at the same time she
fascinated me with her elegance and something else that I

could not recognise but was a suggestion of cruelty. Like the others, I wanted to follow her about all the time. I did often follow her secretly (secretly because I knew she did not like me, and I thought she would despise me for wanting to be with her). But it was not true, as she afterwards accused me, that I was spying on her. That time I was not even following her, it was pure chance that I came across her among the dunes with this young man. They were seated on the ground and she was digging the tip of her parasol in the sand as she talked. I turned and walked away at once, so how could she have thought I was spying on her? She must have seen me in retreat. I never said anything about it to her. And if there was nothing in it why did it matter me mentioning it to Papa?

'We did meet her coming out of church after Evensong with her aunt and the young man. He was tall and rather alarmingly haughty in a willowy aristocratic way, and he managed to bow in my direction without appearing to notice me when she introduced him. His name was Oliver Bridgewater, and he was a cousin of hers, she said. Papa didn't like him either, he called him "a jackanapes". He did not come down again.

'The summer went slowly over. The picture, in a gilt frame too ornate for its pastel tints, hung between the windows in the drawing-room. I learned to put up my long heavy hair. I was eighteen. Miss Falk returned to Town.

'In September Papa went to Switzerland for a month. From time to time we received coloured postcards with affectionately non-committal remarks on the reverse side. It was unlike Papa not to write a proper letter. As a rule when he was away his letters to us were long and full of accurate geographical and historical local-colour. And now there were only these silly, highly-coloured postcards with only Poste Restante addresses. Harry steamed off the stamps for his collection, Lucy copied the views into her album, and I was left with the bald little messages in his small dear hand-writing.

'At the beginning of October I came in one early evening as dusk was falling, with a great bunch of leaves and berries and twigs I had been gathering, to find Cousin Nell waiting for me in the hall with a face like ash.

' "Thank God, you've come," she whispered, grasping me by the arm and pulling me into her sanctum. "The children don't know yet."

'I said in a high breathless voice:

' "Something's happened to Papa!"

' "Yes! Oh, yes! Dear child, you mustn't mind! He will be happier, you know; and it is of his happiness that we must think."

' "He's dead!" I said in a sickening fright.

' "Oh, no, not that!" she cried in a genuine horror of pity. "How could you think it? Not *dead*! Oh, look! Read it for yourself," she begged, thrusting a letter into my hand and putting a handkerchief to her face.

' "Dear Nell," Papa wrote,

' "Miss Falk has done me the honour of becoming my wife. We were married five weeks ago by special licence, and will be returning home on the 7th, arriving on the 5.25. Please see that Thomas is there with the carriage. Sophia is very fond of carnations, will you see that some are in her room? She will use Laura's room of course.

' "I wish you would give these tidings to Blanche Rose for me and she can tell the others in her own way. You, my dear Nell, who have served us all so faithfully, must not feel in any hurry to leave us; you shall suit your own convenience entirely."

'I did not bother to read any more. I crumpled the letter in my hand and stood up.

' "There, dear!" said Cousin Nell, blowing her nose, "I'm sorry to have wept; it was the shock. I'm sure I do hope they'll be very happy. I shall write to Elspeth at once, to ask if I can come to her."

' "You'll not leave us?" I cried, suddenly finding my voice. "You mustn't leave us now! I don't want to be alone with her!"

' "Why, Blanche, dear, you won't be alone with her. And just to begin with of course I'll be here. Your father would expect it of me. He'd think me ungrateful if I turned on my heel now, and I wouldn't want him to know I was hurt by his lack of confidence."

'I knelt down and put my head in her lap to hide my tears.

' "Don't leave us, dear, dear Cousin Nell," I said desperately. "I know I've often been hateful and thoughtless, but I will be better. I didn't understand. I couldn't bear for you to go!"

'I could feel her movement of surprise, but she only said evenly: "It is not possible, dear. You must see that your – that – that – " she sought the word helplessly and then said – "that she will want to run her house in her own way; and there will be no room in it for me. One could not expect it to be otherwise. And it will be better so, you will find; you will all be young people together."

' "Except Papa," I said. "Oh, how could he have done it? How could he, at his age?" I cried bitterly, and my heart was sick with disgust.

' "You are too young to understand these things. You must think only of his happiness, Blanche."

' "But what about mine?" I cried childishly. "What about mine?" '

CHAPTER THREE

'I hope I am not boring you,' Miss Hine suddenly broke off to say.

'Not at all,' he assured her politely. 'But do you mind if I smoke?' For now that the meal was over he was feeling at the same time sleepy and fidgety, and his hostess had become aware of the slight restless movements he made with his legs and shoulders.

'Smoke by all means,' the old lady said, 'but not, I sincerely hope, one of those brief unfragrant machine-made affairs that epitomise for me all the horrors of our ersatz civilisation.' (Mr Jones furtively slid his cigarette-case back inside his jacket and made a mental note of the *chic* of her disapprobation.) 'Have you ever tried a hookah? If not, do me the pleasure of trying one now, and I think you will agree that it is more agreeable than the fusty inhalations of your little adulterated tubes of paper.'

A servant in answer to her summons brought in the mechanism and lit it, and Miss Hine demonstrated to him how it was used. When it began to bubble he drew in the fragrant smoke and presently found himself pleasantly soothed and trancey. He was suddenly aware that he was enjoying this unwonted experience, and his irritation at the enforced loss of time spent listening to this prosy old lady's meandering story of her far-away youth all vanished away and a drowsy contentment took its place.

The old lady continued, folding her plump brown hands again loosely in her lap.

'As soon as Papa and my stepmother returned I saw that Cousin Nell was right, she could not stay. Sophia meant her to go and showed it plainly with a cruel sweetness of manner that pretended she was reluctantly falling in with Cousin Nell's own wishes. And when Papa declared that Nell must be in no hurry to leave them, must stay with them at least another month or two, Sophia gently interpolated, "But, Edward dear, you don't understand. Cousin Nell will have made her arrangements and will be longing to get away and lead her own life. We must not be selfish and put our interests above her own. Men never understand these things, do they?" she said, turning to Cousin Nell with her pretty tinkling laugh.

'And Cousin Nell with more wit than I expected answered smoothly that at any rate one could always rely on another woman to understand. Sophia smiled. And that was that. But Cousin Nell was deeply wounded, we all cried when she left and our easy tears sprung her own. Sentiment, I suppose you'd say; but we were sorry now to think we had ever been ungrateful and unkind. The young have such an abiding sense of justice; so that even Harry, who was boyishly enchanted with his stepmother, felt the injustice of it, yet was glad to have Sophia presiding as the goddess of the home.

'I suppose it was natural enough to her, but I found it unforgivable that Sophia's first step was to redecorate the house that still bore for us the imprint of Mama's personality. The crape was whisked away, and there appeared new crimson carpet and walls of *eau-de-nil* satin paper or french-grey, with gilt-framed mirrors everywhere. It was much prettier, much gayer, and I detested it with all my heart. I, at least, would continue to wear mourning.

'I must admit she was always kind to Harry and surprisingly tolerant, considering the way he used to follow her about. I think she found him amusing with his high spirits and his devotion. She would always find time to pose for his photographs, which was something Lucy and I found inexpressibly irksome. In those days posing meant remaining absolutely motionless for minutes together, there were no "instantaneous" photographs. Yet he was always developing pictures of her in some languid attitude in a basket-chair, or admiring a fall of wistaria, the lines of her dress a serene contrast against the trellis. Apart from the gratification of her vanity, I think she liked to tease Papa with Harry, using the boy deliberately to make Papa aware of her power over him. Consciously or no, she set us all against one another. For instance, Papa would come into a room and find Harry and his stepmother laughing together, and sharply order the boy upstairs to brush his hair or something, and Harry would flush and Sophia would pat his cheek in silent commiseration and see from the corner of her eye my father fume. As for me, I detested to see Papa's eyes following her about always with that hungry look; he reminded me of Floss, our spaniel, who was so quickly cowed it was sometimes painful to see; they had the same darkly speaking eyes. Even in front of us he could not keep his hands from touching her, her body was like a magnet to him all the time, drawing him with its white aloof beauty. And she gave nothing. She was the Ice Maiden. Only sometimes I would see her eyes rest on him with a quiet smile and he would stir uneasily and the expression in his own eyes would make me look away in shame. I hated her for making him look like that. And I honestly think my hatred amused her as much as Harry's admiration. I have already said that I was self-conscious and gauche, and it pleased her to seek out all my sore little spots of unconfidence and call my attention to them in public as dulcetly as one could imagine. At the end of an afternoon's tea-party I would feel as full of pin-pricks as a dressmaker's dummy and not half so handsome or useful.

'Yet I was astonished when she began discussing my future with Papa. Her plan was to rent a house in Town for "the season" and "bring me out". The mere idea was disagreeable to me beyond words; if I dreaded the ordeal of "coming out", I dreaded even more the idea of being perpetually in Sophia's company. But my opinion was not of course asked, although I was obliged to be present and attend this humiliating discussion, with Sophia's sweet sharp decisions cutting through Papa's irritable refusal to see any need for such senseless waste of money.

' "She is eighteen," Sophia said, "and we must do something for the poor child." (She always called me "the poor child".) "What will become of her otherwise? I am not going to pretend that it will be easy to find her a husband, but it seems to me no more than our duty to do what we can for the poor child, unless you are prepared to have her on your hands for the rest of your life," and she gave Papa that demurely intimate and secretive little smile of hers that seemed to say, "You know all I want is to be alone with you."

' "I cannot afford it. It means keeping up two establishments; and who will look after the other children?"

' "But, Edward, don't you see that it is for your convenience?" she said in an impatient undertone. "As for this place, we can shut it up for a few months and take the other children with us, it will do them no harm. I shall prefer to have them under my eye. You see how seriously I take my duties towards my stepchildren, Mr Sheridan? They need a mother's watchful care at their age, you have no idea how abominably sly girls are in their teens,' she said, as if I were not present.

'Papa promised to think about it.

'Sophia demurely turned away her eyes and said, "Also my consideration is that my dear husband will be spared his tiring railway journey twice a day, and will return to me sooner every evening. Weigh that in the balance too, Edward, won't you?"

'They sent me away then, and, grown girl though I was, I scrambled up the heights of the cedar of Lebanon and there in its private shade considered the tormenting problem of the future. What did puzzle me immensely was why Sophia should go to all this trouble, for I knew it did mean a lot of trouble, for my sake. I thought perhaps the London-bred Miss Falk found she could not be happy in the country, and the town-house was to be the thin end of a wedge. I should hate to live in a city, I knew; even the thought of a "season", of dinner parties and balls, filled me with terror. I should never learn how to talk to men, and I certainly did not want to be taught by Sophia with her smarmy sneery ways that made one feel now hot, now cold, which I had so quickly learnt to dread. I prayed fervently that this particular cup of gaiety would pass from me.

'But that was not to be. And presently I heard Father talking about a house in Kensington Gore. My heart sank. "Oh, Papa, please not," I said involuntarily. Papa looked vexed and I hastily stared down at my plate so that he should not see my unhappy face.

'I did not get another chance of pleading with him until the next Sunday on our way to church for Evensong, because Sophia had stayed at home with a headache. Lucy and Harry walked ahead of us, and I began to wish I had not secretly asked them to, I felt so ill at ease with Papa. It occurred to me with a little shock that this was actually the first time I had been alone with him since his re-marriage. I suppose we had both been avoiding one another. I was always afraid he would talk to me about Sophia. Only necessity had obliged me now to confront him and I was surprised by the turmoil it aroused in my bosom, the conflict of my jealous hatred and my jealous love. I found myself sunk into an awkward silence . . . Everything was bathed in the golden glow of the setting sun, the cottages and fields shared impartially the same benign influence. I heard a curlew's bubbling cry rise up. I clenched my fingers over my prayer-book, hard, and said quickly: "Papa, need I go to London?" He woke from his thoughts and looked at me absently.

'He said in a not pleased voice: "What can you be thinking of, Blanche Rose? You know very well we are only going to all this trouble and expense for your sake."

' "I should so very much rather not, Papa."

'He told me how lucky I was, how grateful I should be,

how exceedingly kind it was of Sophia to do all this for me. I must do my part and show that I appreciated it. I must try and be more of a companion to Sophia, who after all was only like an elder sister to me, she was scarcely more than a child just out of the schoolroom herself, only twenty-four now, the dear plucky girl, he said.

'I heard what he said but my heart and mind were inexorably shut. I said: "Papa, please don't make me Come Out, I should hate it so awfully!"

'He said sternly: "No more of this, Blanche. You will make me annoyed. In any event, it is too late now for the decision to be reversed, the house is rented."

'I could feel myself go white. I stopped, and the beckoning bell was noisy in my head. I said in a low faltering voice: "Papa, I beseech you . . . " But he would not hear any more. The church in the distance and the tiny dark people moving along the road banked with grass were all blurred with my tears, tears I would not let fall. "I shall never marry!" I promised him with bitter defiance.

'He stopped too and faced me then. The bell had ceased. And in the sudden peaceful silence he said, "My dear daughter, I think you will do well to reconsider that decision. The alternative if you do not marry will be to remain at home with your stepmother and me for the rest of your life. Had you thought of that?" He turned and walked on, and I followed him in a daze.

'I made no more protest. I had not somehow realised that he would be married to Sophia for ever. Now in my mind the shadowy usurper took my place and I became the interloper. No, Papa was right, I did not want to stay at home, year after year, dwindling into Sophia's butt, the dowdy, unwanted, unmarried daughter.

'So I came to Town and spent many tedious hours in fitting-rooms and many tedious afternoons driving with Sophia in our hired barouche from one house to another in Belgravia and Cadogan Square to make our fifteen-minute calls.

'The house in Kensington Gore was heavily furnished in the old-fashioned style that reminded me of The Grange when Mama was alive; I obstinately liked its stuffy hangings. I had very little time to myself, very little time to spend with Lucy and Harry in the schoolroom thinking up "larks". London made them listless too; or perhaps it was just that they were growing up. Usually I went to see them when Sophia's cousin, Oliver Bridgewater, came to talk business with her, mostly, I believe, about Sophia's mother, who lived by herself somewhere in South London. At any rate, I always was glad to escape for a while. Mr Bridgewater's affectation of superiority and boredom alarmed me. He was indifferent even to Sophia, who treated him just as carelessly back. He came often to the house now, was invited to all Sophia's little dinner parties (where he was usually obliged to be nothing more exciting than my dinner-partner), and sometimes would accompany us on our drives. It struck me that although they were obliged to see so much of each other, they were really antagonistic. They spoke curtly and coldly to one another, like polite enemies, and took care to avoid one another's eyes.

'The season started, and I began to be invited to balls. That meant hours of having my hair frizzed out unbecomingly with the tongs and crammed agonisingly with pins to keep it in place. I was dressed absurdly in girlish white muslins, in which I looked ridiculous, but they were considered to be "so suitable, so appropriate" to a young girl, that it was useless for me to question it. But I resented being made to look a fool and showed it in my sullen unhappy face. And almost every day there was this ordeal to be gone through; and Sophia would never allow me to leave before 2 a.m. It was strictly understood that even if I was not enjoying myself we must give the impression that I was. For me a ball was made up of *mauvais quarts d'heures* leaning against a wall watching the dancers with a brilliant smile on my aching cheeks. When I did have the luxury of a partner it was not much better. I was no good at dancing, much too stiff and hesitating (except when I danced by myself in the garden at home or in the attics in an unaccustomed ecstasy of spirits). And I could never master the mysteries of small-talk. There was nevertheless one dancing-partner I could rely on to rescue me if things got too bad: Oliver Bridgewater always asked me for a certain number of dances, if only he were there. It was also something of a relief that he did not expect me to talk, he preferred, I think, to dance in silence. Twice he took me down to supper when he saw I had not been engaged for the supper-dance. I could not but feel grateful to him even though I still did not like him much.

'I had never asked myself why he troubled to dance with me so often; since he never looked other than supremely disenthralled, I imagined it was to oblige Sophia that he paid me this duty. It made it the more astounding therefore when one evening he suddenly took both my hands in his and said, a trifle breathlessly, "Blanche Rose, will you – could you marry me?" I drew my hands sharply away and flushed. I thought he was jesting.

'He said:

' "I mean it."

'I could feel tears of shock pricking my eyes. I said:

' "I don't know. I've never thought about it. I had no idea. I don't think I could."

' "Don't answer now," he said. "Think it over, Blanche Rose, please. I should do my best to make you happy."

' "It is an honour, I know," I muttered, fingering the ruching on my muslin skirt. "I'm sorry, I don't know what else to say." There was something so bitterly disappointing to me about my first proposal that my heart felt squeezed down into my satin slippers, so profoundly and painfully had it sunk.

'I escaped from him and found my stepmother, and told her I wanted to leave, I said I was not feeling well. I thought she looked at me oddly, but she said nothing. We drove home in silence.

'Suddenly I burst out against the rumble of wheels:

' "Oliver has asked me to marry him!"

' "And what did you answer?" asked my stepmother apparently unsurprised.

' "I couldn't," I said desperately. "I said I couldn't. Well, how can I?"

' "You must please yourself, of course," she shrugged. "But I should hardly have thought you could afford to turn down a serious offer just for some girlish whim." She looked at me switftly from the corner of her eye. "One has to admit you have not so far been a wild success, my poor child."

' "Which makes me wonder all the more what he wants to marry me *for*."

' "To begin with a rising young barrister needs a suitable wife. A really clever girl can be of great use to her husband, seeing to it that he meets the sort of people he needs to know."

' "He doesn't love me."

' "My poor child, what do you know about it?"

' "He's never – I can't describe what I mean – he's never said anything, the way I imagine men do," I stumbled.

' "I daresay he's too shy. He wouldn't want to frighten you. Besides, you know, that's not the whole of marriage." She looked out of the window at the gas-lamps on the kerb. "Sometimes love can wreck a marriage," she remarked.

'In my room that night I undressed and then for hours paced the floor trying to resolve the situation wisely. It is true, after that conversation with Papa, I had vowed to marry the first man who asked me – since he might well be the only one. But now that it came to the point, I shrank from the plunge. It is true that I had always found Oliver rather intimidating, but perhaps that was mainly because of his association with Sophia. Certainly I liked him much better now that I knew he liked me. And he must at least *like* me to want to marry me. That he had appeared so often to ignore me I must now put down to shyness. It made him easier to understand. He would be, I supposed, considered rather handsome in his unrugged way, with his insolent green eyes and the beautiful pale bow of his mouth. He was reputed to be brilliant but idle in his profession. He had just finished "eating his dinners" in the Temple, and was helping to prepare briefs in someone's Chambers. A wife behind him would cure him of his indolence, I thought. I sat hunched on the bed with my arms wrapped about my knees. I would have my own home. I would be free of Sophia. I would no longer have to endure the sight of Papa being pleasantly tormented by her, nor be tortured myself by the perpetual realisation that she – the witch-stepmother – had supplanted me in his heart. I stretched myself out on the bed and fell instantly asleep.

'I thought the carnations that arrived the next day were for Sophia, but they were for me with a note tucked in them from Oliver. I told the maid to put them in water and turned away, almost ready to change my mind. He came that evening. When I saw him there, slim and bareheaded with his silk hat in his hand, I hesitated. Then I forced myself to go up to him and thank him for the flowers.

'He bowed gravely.

' "I hope you were pleased with them," he said.

'I said, very much aware of my ungraciousness: "I don't like carnations. Please never send me them again." ' (Though the significance of their message had totally escaped me.)

' "How remiss of me not to have realised that. Forgive me, Blanche Rose; I should of course have sent you white roses. May I send you some as a peace-offering?" he said quite charmingly, with his rare smile.

'I smiled back at him shyly.

'We stood there for what seemed to me a long while in silence. And he looked at me as if he were seeing me for the first time. I was wretchedly conscious of my ill-dressed hair and my stern unprovocative features, I knew my solemn young face was already too full of character for the taste of the period, but I held my head proudly high and bore his scrutiny as well as I could. Then, unexpectedly, he leaned forward and turned my face to his and kissed my mouth. It was the first time I had ever been kissed on the mouth, and I found the cool firm pressure of his lips not unpleasant; but I was less aware of that, in the confusion of my thoughts and my racing heart, than of his silk hat bowling in half a circle across the tessellated floor to the feet of the parlourmaid, who stooped and picked it up with a sly expression, which, though she tried to conceal it, said to me as plainly as words: "Fancy, Miss Blanche! *That* plain thing!" I was horribly ashamed. I knew that "fast" girls sometimes allowed themselves to be kissed, and I had no idea how far I was committed by it. In my pathetic ignorance I believed I now was trapped. I drew away from him sharply, angrily humiliated.

' "You shouldn't have done that," I stormed. "You had no right. It was mean! I meant to tell you later; you said you'd wait." '

'He gave an amused exclamation. "A prickly white rose, he said. "Was I expected to ask permission to kiss you? If I had, you would only have said No, wouldn't you?"

' "Not if we were engaged," I said.

'He picked up my hand. "But we can be, as soon as you say so and your father gives his consent. I thought you were going to refuse me. Why did you look so angry and frighten me, cruel girl?" he said with his small sardonic smile.

' "You are so unexpected," I complained. "I never dreamed you were going to propose. You've always been so – never noticing me. I don't know why you should want to marry me."

' "Why do you imagine men ever marry girls, my innocent little rose?"

' "I suppose because they love them," I said soberly. "But I don't think you love me, do you?"

' "Why else should I want to marry you?" he answered.

'I could not understand this. But what did I know about love? I said unsteadily, "Then – then are we engaged?"

' "I believe we are," he said with a mocking seriousness to match my own.

'And we were.'

CHAPTER FOUR

A MARRIAGE HAS BEEN ARRANGED

'I found being engaged pleasant but bewildering. I was considered notably more important now and I was asked for my opinion just as if I were an adult. It was evidently regarded as a triumph for the Ugly Duckling, and I was not much used to being admired. I was disconcerted by this unlooked-for approval, I had the uneasy feeling that I was being commended for something I had not even tried to accomplish,' said old Miss Hine with irony.

'Not that the course of true love ran as smoothly as that implies. To begin with Papa refused his consent. His first impulse was to banish Oliver from the house. He was not, Papa said firmly, a suitable *parti*. He was not the husband Papa wanted for his daughter at all . . . a man who had still his way to make in the world and who was quite unable to provide for a wife.

' "He is not the right person to make you happy," Papa said.

' "I should at any rate be happier than living at home with you and Stepmama," I said hardly.

' "My child," Papa said in a low voice. "You do not know what marriage is. You cannot know the wretchedness of an unhappy marriage."

'I said stubbornly that I saw no reason why it should be unhappy. I wanted to marry Oliver, I was immensely proud that he should want to marry me, and Papa's unfairness only stiffened my resolve. Without it, I might have weakened from fright and backed out. But indignation was like starch in my veins, stiffening me. I summoned angry tears.

'Papa said gently, "When you are older and happily married to the right person, you will thank me. I'm not denying young Bridgewater has charm and good looks and so forth, but that is not enough in a husband. He must be able to provide for his family as well, you know; and I'm bound to say I have no confidence in his abilities."

' "Everyone says Oliver is brilliant," I said hotly.

' "He is twenty-seven. Time he stopped showing promise and produced results."

' "You don't like him," I said with a queer sort of triumph. "You don't like him!" And indeed the realisation of this filled me with savage delight. I was glad Papa did not want me to marry him, I was glad he did not like Oliver, I was glad to think my marriage would make him unhappy. This was paying skin for skin! It was now in my power, I saw, to hurt my father as much as he had hurt me. If anything could have fixed my obstinate determination to marry Oliver it was my exultant awareness of Papa's disapprobation.

' "My dear, it is not for me to like or dislike him: I have not got to marry him," he said patiently. "I have only to see that my daughter does not fall into the hands of the wrong kind of man."

' "You *told* me to find myself a husband and now that I have found one you say he is the wrong kind," I said sulkily.

' "My child, if you really are fond of this man," he said guilefully, "you will understand that it is not being fair to him to marry him. To have a young family to fend for would be a cruel handicap to him at the beginning of his career. He should marry a girl with a fortune of her own."

' "Oliver's not a fortune-hunter!" I said scornfully and triumphantly.

' "Perhaps not,' said Papa doubtfully. "It is certain that you have no fortune of your own; yet how are you to live if I do not provide for you? Oliver has no money at all."

' "He must have some!"

' "He has no money at all. Nothing – beyond what he earns. And I have made enquiries. He idles. In the last year, I understand, he has been given opportunities in three sets of Chambers and on each occasion, after a few months, he has fallen away. He makes about enough to pay for his cab fares, I should judge. I wonder if you have any conception, my poor Blanche, of the bills young men of his type run up at their tailors and hatters and wine-merchants? Very well, then, who is to finance all this? Your father, who has three other children still to educate and provide for and a wife to keep? It may even be – though this is not a subject I care to discuss with a young unmarried daughter," Papa said hurriedly with a look of dark embarrassment, "yet it may even be that God will bless us . . . that you will have other brothers and sisters, I mean," he concluded lamely.

' "It's not my fault that you married again! Why should my life be made wretched because you and Stepmama . . . because you may have other children besides us? We came first."

'He had been standing with his back to the fire with his coat-tails parted, arguing with me patiently, so maddeningly sure of himself; but these words struck an anger from his heart to equal my own. I quailed. This was my stern Papa of long ago that I feared and revered and loved.

'He said in a quiet terrible voice, "Go to your room, miss! I'll hear no more of this. And I will tolerate no more of this nonsense about getting married."

'I went meekly enough, but inwardly the injustice of it brought me out in a rash of rebellion, in which curiously enough, I was encouraged and supported by, of all people, Sophia. It was strange to find my old enemy fighting on my side. But without her I should never have got my way. I believe she wanted me to marry Oliver. Perhaps it was that she wanted to get this great sullen girl out of the house for good and all. (There would still be Lucy to marry off after that, but she was a pretty, docile, amenable child.) Oh, there is no doubt of it, it was Sophia who somehow prevailed on my father to change his mind, by what arts I know not.

'Papa's idea was a grudging consent stipulating a long, a very long, engagement. I think even Sophia would have been hard put to it to wangle out of that. But Papa had rather suddenly to go abroad and Sophia was to go with him of course. There was some trouble in the tea gardens in Ceylon or Burma, I forget which. In any case, while he was out there he would visit them all. He would be gone several months, perhaps even as long as a year.

'Sophia insisted that I should be married first. (We had returned to Essex directly Papa refused Oliver my hand, so that I should not be encouraged by seeing him. Afterwards, when the engagement was permitted, he did come down sometimes, and Sophia sat in the room with us and helped us make conversation. I cannot remember that he ever kissed me again, except in front of Sophia when he put the ruby on my finger, until after we were married.) I mention this to show you how conventual was the upbringing of delicate maidens in the far off days of my youth.

'Sophia refused to take the responsibility of leaving me in England with no suitable elder person to look after me. The idea of my being alone in a room with my fiancé and no one to chaperon me apparently outraged her sense of decency. It would never do, she assured Papa. What would people say? And girls were so sly, they were simply not to be trusted. And then if anything should occur later to prevent the marriage my good name would be ruined and my chances spoilt for ever.

'Whereas, she pointed out with some cunning, if we were already married we could perfectly well start our housekeeping at The Grange, which would be convenient for us and at the same time I could mind my brothers and sister. Thus saving Papa the trouble of looking for an elderly person as reliable as Cousin Nell, and the expense of keeping her.

'There was some conflict in my mind over that. I did by

now desperately want to be married and have done with it.
On the other hand, quite an important factor to me in my
marriage was the prospect of getting away from The
Grange with all its old associations, getting away from
Papa, from Sophia, from all that now meant home to me. I
candidly hated the idea of beginning my married life in The
Grange, it seemed dreadfully inauspicious. Yet what could
I say? I must either let Sophia have her way in this or in
nothing, and leave my engagement to trail miserably along
for years. Of course I backed her up, of course I said I could
quite well look after Lucy and Harry and Edgar, of course I
said I wanted to get married immediately; and indeed I was
thankful for the chance of a small quiet country wedding.

'So Oliver and I were married and went to Venice for our
honeymoon. We were to return to The Grange when Papa
and Sophia sailed.

'It is a wonder to me how any marriage survives the
honeymoon – that season of disillusion and boredom.
Perhaps if one is truly in love one can survive the experience
of the barbaric cruelty of being, as it were, rejected from
society and driven together like unhappy exiles for this
period. As though it could ever be a pleasure for two strangers to be forced to live together in the closest intimacy
night and day without even the relief of another person's
presence. Oliver and I, at any rate, were complete strangers
to each other and knew nothing of what the other liked or
disliked. I was wretchedly ill at ease with him. I did not
know what husbands and wives were supposed to talk
about when they were together. He made very little effort at
amusing me, and appeared either languidly indifferent, or
lost in sombre thought. He would answer all my questions
about the splendours around us most courteously, but he
did not trouble to point them out to me if they escaped my
notice.

'I imagined miserably that I had failed him in some way,
that he already regretted having married me. I wanted
above all things to honour my side of the contract, since he

had given me the chance to escape from under Sophia's hand. It never occurred to me to ask myself whether I loved him; I had been brought up to believe that wives always did love their husbands – automatically, as it were – and husbands their wives; that love was wrought by the miracle of marriage. If I had not been sure of my feelings before marriage I took it for granted that I loved him now.

'How infinitely pathetic young people are,' sighed the old woman. 'It is such an old story, always the same, and always new to the one it happens to. That malevolent little piece of paper which the wife finds.' She lifted her hands a little and let them fall again into her capacious lap. 'It occurred one evening when I had gone to my room to change for dinner. Oliver had changed first and gone downstairs again, for I had had a letter to write. His jacket was lying in a heap on the floor, he was hopelessly untidy, and I picked it up and gave it a little shake to straighten it. I did not go over his pockets. I should not have dreamed of such a thing. The paper fluttered out when I shook it. Even then I might not have noticed it if the pretty florid handwriting had not caught my eye. I thought, how funny of Oliver never to mention to me that he had heard! I stooped for it. The words "darling Noll" sprang out at me irresistibly, and I saw the paper shake in my hand. The terror of the words lay in their unfamiliarity; I had never heard her call anyone darling, not even my father; nor had she ever called Oliver "Noll" in my hearing.

'I crossed to the door and turned the key in the lock. Then I deliberately unfolded the letter.

'I had never received a love-letter in my life, so how did I know that this was one? There was not a word of love in it. Except that the run of laconic cynical phrases were broken suddenly by: *"Oh, my darling Noll!"* like a cry of anguish wrung from the ache of her longing and desperately scrawled across the page. And then she instantly resumed her light manner. She took herself up for that moment of weakness. She refused to rail at Fate over their hard lot, she declared. Fate was nothing but an old curmudgeon invented by cowards to excuse their lack of enterprise. She was not to be scared by bogeys. Had she not been admirably clever so far? she demanded. He must be patient, patient, patient; she knew what she was doing, and were not his interests her own? It was signed satirically, his devoted "Cousin" in inverted commas, no more. But I knew who it was from, of course, it did not need her signature.'

Lancelot Jones, who liked to be certain of his facts, murmured:

'I suppose it *was* from Sophia?'

'Have you not been attending?' said the old lady testily, as if he were a dull or idle schoolboy and she the teacher. 'Of course it was from Sophia. It is curious to think that if she had not signed herself "Cousin" like that, I might never have known they were not really related.'

'Oh, come!' he protested. 'People do, you know, sometimes address one another with extreme formality when they are really intimate. I think it was rather jumping to conclusions to assume that they were not cousins at all. I mean, why should they say they were if they were not?'

'Can't you imagine?' said the old lady sardonically. 'Do you think I was making up a situation out of nothing?'

'I'm bound to say that if you had no other evidence than the letter to go on, I think you were interpreting it rather hysterically.'

'How do you make that out?' she said surprised.

'I take it you believed your husband and your stepmother were lovers,' he said.

'Oh, heavens *no!*' exclaimed the old woman, throwing up her hands in pious horror. 'Of course I didn't. What would a girl of eighteen – in Victorian times – know of such things? It could never have entered my head – I had only been married three weeks, and I still did not know what the seventh Commandment meant. No, all I imagined was that they were in love. And that was quite terrible enough for me, I do assure you.

'I sat, I remember, for a long time staring out of the bed-room window at the darkening canal and the lights pricking out above it one by one and sending long yellow streamers wavering across the dark oily water. At last I folded up the little scrap of paper and tucked it back inside his jacket and hung it away – out of sight but never again out of mind. Then I rang for the *valet de chambre* and sent him with a message to my husband, that I would not be down to dinner, I had a headache. I wanted time to think, you see. I wanted to get the whole thing clear in my mind. I wanted to decide what had to be done. Oddly enough, it was less of myself than of Papa I was thinking. If I had tears to shed they should be for him; but I had none, I felt as dry-eyed and hard as a stone.

'I had wanted to be revenged on Papa, but I had not meant anything like this, not anything that would *break* him. I knew, I had *seen*, with what wretched abandon he had given Sophia his heart. I suppose he never was really sure that she loved him back. How could he be? But to know that she had never loved him and was in love with someone else would be an irrecoverable blow. I realised then that this knowledge must for ever be kept to myself. Not only could I not run with it to Papa, but I must shield him from ever learning anything about it.'

Mr Jones stood up and surreptitiously rubbed his cramped muscles. He moved stiffly across to the window and leaned his elbows in the embrasure. In the courtyard below he could see a servant in a striped vest, with a grimy turban coiled loosely round his head, squatting on his hams before a charcoal brazier and blowing it red.

Lancelot said abstractedly, 'You were making a terrific mountain, weren't you, over surely the merest little scrap-heap of paper?'

'Does it seem so to you?' she said. 'There were the carnations, don't forget.'

'Carnations?'

'That Oliver sent me after his proposal. I hated them

because they were Sophia's favourite flower. They were always in stiff little bouquets all over the house. I disliked them because they reminded me of Sophia herself with their prim starchy petticoats so deceptively at variance with their cloying fragrance. Perhaps she only liked them the best of all flowers because they happened to be the ones Oliver gave her. He always did give them to her, and so I suppose without thinking he ordered them for me too. How true, how cynically true, that there is a language of flowers! Those carnations he sent me declared as plainly as words his passion for Sophia, only I did not understand their message till too late.'

But the young man was not listening. He was watching in fascinated horror the man in the courtyard dipping his fingers into the pan on the brazier to savour the quality of the contents. Mr Jones hoped devoutly that it was not something that he was going to be expected to eat. The old woman peered over his shoulder, curious to see what held his attention. Unconscious of his observers, the man in the courtyard fished something black about the size of a walnut out of the pan (not without much difficulty and blowings-on of fingers and licking-off of burning sauce) and popped the tit-bit quickly in his mouth. He chewed it blissfully for a moment and then suddenly spat it into his hand, scrutinised it like an augur inspecting the entrails of an eagle, and in a fit of temperament flung it on the ground and stamped on it.

'That's a good thing!' said the old woman drily. 'I'm glad he found that bit himself. I always say, there are more uses than one for a food-taster.'

'Do you mean we are going to eat that?' said Mr Jones faintly.

'Oh, no. Abdul would never dream of serving up a dish that had anything wrong with it. He is absolutely scrupulous.'

'Scrupulous is scarcely the word I would have chosen,' murmured Mr Jones in the same dying voice. 'Do you think

he ought to be allowed to lick . . . to lick his fingers
. . . and dip them in the pot like that? Doesn't it seem to you
– forgive me for mentioning it – a little unhygienic? I'm
afraid you think me very pernickety.'

'My dear, what is one to do? You see, Abdul learnt
cooking from the chefs in the big European hotels. He is an
excellent cook, but I'm afraid he did pick up a lot of dirty
little habits there. He's not supposed to do the actual
cooking as a rule – that's how I get round it – he just directs
his artless, and therefore cleaner, confrères. But of course
temperament, you know; one cannot prevent the poor
fellow trying out new dishes from time to time. And naturally he delights to show his skill when we are honoured with
a guest,' she observed with bland irony.

But Mr Jones fancied his digestion was delicate, his
palate unusually sensitive, and he shrank from the ordeal as
if it were a form of torture.

'But perhaps the plane will be repaired before then?' he
murmured.

'You would leave without hearing the rest of my tale?'
cried the old woman, piqued.

'Of course not, of course not,' he said hastily, thinking
how obsessed with egotism old people were.

'It doesn't interest you,' she averred, hunching her shoulders like a sulky teddy-bear.

'It does indeed,' he assured her. 'I'm afraid I interrupted
you, but please do go on.'

'No,' she said. 'We'll leave it, damn it! Why should you
care? I'll send someone to see how your pilot's getting on.'
She leaned forward as she passed the opening and gave an
order to the servant who stood in the passage beyond the
archway.

'I do want to hear, I assure you. It is most interesting.' He
sought words. 'Really, it's history – a social history of the
period. Most instructive. How you all thought and so on.'

She gave him a faint mollified smile.

'Very well,' she agreed at last. 'And we shall dispose of

your portion of Abdul's dinner if you do not fancy it, and you shall dine ascetically off goat's milk cheese and fresh figs and watch me wallowing in Abdul's sinister but delectable offerings.'

If he felt a moment's unease at this hint that she had read his thoughts so accurately he quickly decided that it could only have been a random suggestion. He meekly enough resumed his seat and waited for her to resume her tale.

CHAPTER FIVE

THE RETURN

'The thing I could not understand,' recommenced Miss Hine, 'was how Sophia could ever have married Papa when it was Oliver she loved. Since he loved her too, why had she not married Oliver? It seemed so simple and obvious. I used to puzzle over it wearily, poor simpleton that I was. I never imagined that anything so trivial as penury could have kept them apart. But then it was only an abstract word to me, and I had no idea what it meant. Girls hadn't in those days, if they came from the middle classes. Poverty to me meant taking veal broth into dark noisome cottages with their small leaded windows tightly closed against the dangerous air. Horrible! But nothing to do with US. I did not know about the kind of poverty that means brown paper in the soles of one's shoes, battling with duns, accepting snubs with a bright smile, and paying for life with coppers. If I had known about it I would have understood that that would have meant defeat to Sophia. To undertake a life of petty pricking poverty demands a kind of courage and a kind of love that Sophia could never have. She had courage all right, but it was a hard, brilliant sort of courage that would dare and dare, and dare yet again, provided she could assault life in the confidence of a brave silk dress from the fortress of her impregnably ladylike demeanour. Sophia was always the lady, however despicably she behaved! She wanted money and she was prepared to pay the price for it. She knew what she was doing. It was, after all, perfectly respectable. I am sure she would not have forfeited her precious respectability for any amount of money. It had to be *marriage*. When one puts it like that, one sees how exactly Father fitted the bill. She could hardly hope to aspire higher than a wealthy merchant, after all. The chances and opportunity for her to attract the notice of a young man with money were too slender to count. A widower, on the other hand, was by no means impossible. And in a widower no longer young there were positive advantages. Men as a rule died younger than women. And Father was thirty years older than Sophia. So you see it was not by any means an impossible dream that she would one day be a wealthy widow. Perhaps in five years, perhaps ten. Not surely a great deal of one's life to give to the amassing of a fortune? (It had taken Father considerably longer than that to make it!) And afterwards, the luxury of freedom!

'She would be free to marry again. The positions would be reversed, and she would be the rich widow whose hand would be sought. But Oliver would not be free. She could surely not hope that I, still so young, would conveniently die too. Why had she let Oliver marry me? Why, she had actually encouraged the match and done all she could to bring it about. Perhaps she had even pushed him into it, *told* him to marry me. She must feel very sure that she had nothing to be jealous of in me, I thought bitterly. Perhaps that was the answer.

'She was so positive that Oliver could find nothing to love in me that she actually preferred to see him safely married to me, since she could still continue to see him constantly, than risk losing him to some wealthier, prettier bride, who would carry him off in the body too, away from the sphere of her influence.

'All this sounds as if Oliver was very weak. But he was weak, you know, for all his air of haughty indifference, and I was beginning to understand that he was completely ruled by Sophia. For that matter, what man isn't ruled by some woman?

'For he loathed on principle any form of work. Papa was right about him. He was hopelessly indolent. It shocked my conventional puritan soul to see how contentedly idle he could be, if he had a good cigar and a glass of wine. He looked down on Papa for a tradesman. "I was born an aristocrat," he used to tell me when I remonstrated with him.'

'Yet still I pondered, how did she mean to get rid of me when Papa was dead? I was pretty sure she would not tolerate being just Papa's widow, with Papa's tiresome daughter between her and the man she wanted. And as I have said before, she thought too much of the sanctity of respectability to run away with Oliver, however rich she became. It was a pretty little problem with which to divert oneself in the white hours of the night.

'But I digress. These finer points only troubled my peace later. Immediately after my discovery my chief concern was how I was going to bear seeing them both again. I was afraid of seeing Papa, afraid he would see the unhappiness in my eyes and question me. The nearer came the day of our return, the more I dreaded it. At last by a ruse I evaded the situation. I "lost" my jewel-case and acted a perfect frenzy for Oliver's benefit, which must have made him wonder, seeing me for the first time so unlike myself.

'Anyway, I attained my object; we missed the train that day. We should not be back before Papa's boat sailed. We sent him a wire to say we had been unavoidably detained, not to worry, that we would be home without fail the day after.

'How well I remember that homecoming! So different from what I had expected.

'I had thought the children would be at the station to meet us. Meeting trains was still an exciting adventure in those days. Even apart from that, I thought they would have wanted to see me. The empty grey parallel of platform struck a chill to my heart, as if something had gone wrong, though I told myself that I was being absurd. As we rumbled up the drive, I stared up at the vacant windows. Not even Edgar's baby face at the nursery window. I pressed my hands together and drew back into the dark corner of the carriage to conceal my agitation.

'It seemed an age before the parlourmaid answered my ring.

' "Good afternoon, Miss – M'm, that is. Welcome 'ome," she said nervously.'

'I stood in the hall stripping off my gloves and trying not to shiver.

' "Where is everyone?" I said lightly. "Are they all well?"

'She cast a look over her shoulder.

' "Oh, yes, M'm, quite well, if you please," she said with a ridiculous sort of bob.

' "Tea, Beulah, in the drawing-room. Is the fire alight? I'm cold."

' "Very good, M'm," she said, with a scared look that yet struck me as having something exultant in it, the sort of pleasurable horror one feels at the really gruesome moment of a ghost story. I fancied that I must be imagining things, and what with the sense of inward chill I began to think I must be going to be ill. I suddenly realised what was making me feel sick was the smell of carnations. There was a bowl of them, yellow and white, on the console table in the hall, stuck stiffly in a little object full of holes like an umbrella stand.

'I said, "Take those flowers with you and throw them away," in a cold voice.

' "Oh, but what a pity, when they were put there specially to welcome you!" exclaimed an amused voice lightly behind me.

'I turned.

' "Why, you look as white as a pillar of salt! Aren't you pleased to see me?" said Sophia with her little ringing laugh.

'The children rushed out at me, chanting, "Surprise! Surprise!" and buffeting me affectionately.

' "Lucy! Harry! Where's Papa, then? Hasn't he gone?" I asked bewildered.

' "Oh, yes, he's gone, he's gone. And we all went to Tilbury to see him off." They were laughing with excitement and talking so hard that I could not follow. From the corner of my eye I was watching Sophia, serenely smiling in a dress of olive-green velvet.

' "And how is my stepson-in-law?" I heard her ask my husband.

' "Then why are you still here?" I interrupted rudely.

' "I've not been well. The doctor advised me it would not be wise to accompany your father at present," she said blandly.

'I drew back and took Oliver's arm.

' "You look all right. Doesn't she, Oliver? What's wrong with you?"

' "Really, Blanche, how can you be so stupid?" she cried, impatient and laughing. "Nobody would think you a married woman."

' "Oh!" I said, staring at her with my mouth unbecomingly agape. "You mean, you're – "

'Her sharply raised eyebrows stopped me with their unspoken reproof: "Not before the children!" and I stammered out: "Then you won't be going at all?"

'She agreed, studiedly intent on her white fingers re-arranging the fall of ecru lace at her throat.

' "Then – then – Oliver and I had best return to London."

' "To London?" said my husband, surprised. "My dear Blanche, whatever for?"

' "We can't stay here," I said quickly. "There's no need for it since Stepmama is here."

' "But why not stay here?" said Oliver. "We have nowhere else to go."

' "I don't want to. I never wanted to come back and begin my married life here. I want – "

' "I wouldn't for the world try to persuade Blanche Rose to stay against her will," Sophia said smoothly. "But need we stand in the hall discussing it? You look so cold and tired, Blanche Rose," she said pityingly, with a look that made me feel how plain and pinched and dishevelled I must be. "Come and warm yourself. There's a fire in the drawing-room, and here is Beulah with tea."

'It was over tea that Sophia reminded Lucy to give me the letter Papa had left for me. It was to ask me to look after Sophia in her delicate condition. He was so relieved to think she would not be without the solace of another woman's company. He might not be back until the child was born. And poor little Sophia had been so brave about letting him go. Would I punctiliously write by every mail and report on her health?

'So I settled down glumly into my old life. Oh, the boredom of it, with nothing to do! For I was not allowed to practise running a house, as I had hoped, since Sophia was there to do it. If ever I gave an occasional order contrary to hers, the maids were too afraid of her to obey me. Lucy was still in the schoolroom. Harry went up to Town every day to the business, fancying himself in Papa's place. And Oliver went to the Inner Temple and did whatever barristers do when they're looking for work. There was no company for me all day but Sophia's. She used to follow me into the hall every morning, ostensibly to say good-bye to Harry, while I was finding Oliver's hat and gloves and cane. I would give him a dutiful peck, while Sophia, as if in mockery, would put her hands on Harry's shoulders and gently kiss his cheek and murmur, "Good-bye, dear boy!" And poor Harry would crimson and bolt after Oliver into the landau. How I would long to go with them, out of this house that was no longer home to me, to escape from the boredom of my days!

'I used to walk over the marshes for hours among the scattered sheep, with the clouds blowing across the immense sky like rags. It was the only way I could escape from her presence. Otherwise we took our meals together, and sat together with our books or our sewing in silence. I have often wondered whether she detested it as much as I did.

'I liked best to take my walk when the sun was setting, the

glory added a brightness to my empty day, and later the pensive twilight suited my mood. Once I returned barely half an hour after I set out, for a pin to fasten a broken garter. I ran upstairs. I was so startled to see Oliver on the dusky landing like an apparition that I gave a little cry. His face was white as china.

'He said sharply, "Blanche, what are you doing here?"

'I was taken aback by his tone, but I tartly answered his question with another: "What are you doing here, if it comes to that?"

' "I came back early." He put his hand to his forehead. "I was not feeling very well. I was looking for you when you startled me."

' "Did you expect to find me in Stepmama's room?"

' "I simply . . . I was going to . . . I went to ask her if she knew what had become of you. That was all."

' "What else could there be?" I said.

'Sophia came out of her room with a wrap gathered across her bosom and her red hair falling round her shoulders. I thought it indelicate of her to have appeared *en deshabille* before my husband. I suppose I looked shocked, for she said quickly, "What is the matter? You disturbed me. I was lying down. I am unwell."

' "Dear me!" I said. "Both of you! How unfortunate! Poor Stepmama, should I loosen your stays and put a vinegar compress on your head?"

'When she was angry a flush stained the beauty of her throat. I saw it now and was wickedly glad. I thought it was my remark about the stays that had annoyed her. I knew it was vulgar of me. Moreover, though I modestly tried not to look, it was quite plain that she had already removed them; I could tell by the free way her body moved under the silk wrap. I felt a pang of envy at her pretty figure, so much more elegant than my rangy slouch; one would never have guessed, I thought with astonishment, that she expected a child in five months' time.

'She turned and went back to her room without a word

and shut the door. And Oliver stammered out that he had got such a frightful headache he thought he would come for a walk with me, the air might do him good. He was amazingly affable on the way and I suppose he found me silent, though that was not unusual, but presently he asked me what was the matter, why was I so silent? I said, I never liked to talk when I was walking, but then *I* never wanted to talk when I had a headache either.

'It was soon after that that Oliver got work with a Queen's Counsel, helping prepare the defence for some big trial. He did not trouble to explain it to me, and women in those days rarely bothered to read the papers. He did say that it would mean a lot of very hard work, that it would often necessitate working so late at night that he would not be able to get home. He would stay in Town and dig-in with a friend of his.

'The first week he only spent two nights away from home out of five. Sophia still complained of not feeling well. And in the middle of the second week she decided to go to London to consult a specialist. She travelled up in the care of my brother and husband. She was to return in the evening, but instead came a wire to say: "Specialist insists remain London nursing-home writing."

'I missed the mail to Papa, waiting for that letter. (I could hardly have written to him and not told him Sophia was unwell.) Her letter never came. I thought, perhaps she was too ill to write. I did not know the address of the nursing-home and I did not even know who the specialist was. I blamed myself now for my lack of sympathy. I dreaded Papa's wrath if he should ever find out. I did not know what to do and there was no one to advise me. Oliver all this while was in Town under pressure of work.

'On the sixth day of Oliver's absence a box came for me from a West End florist and inside lay a posy of white roses on a bed of moss. "Never absent from my thoughts. O." he had written on the card. Lucy saw me blush and asked me who they were from. "How dull!" she pouted, when I told her, which made me laugh. "Oh, it's nice," she said. "It is nice without *her!*"

' "I thought you liked her?" I said, absorbed in decapitating my breakfast egg.

' "Well, I do when she's there. She makes you like her," the honest child explained. "So I thought I did. But I like it much better without her. Don't you wish she wouldn't come back?"

'I said demurely, "Papa would not like that."

' "Nor would Harry. Aren't men *silly?*"

' "Does Harry like her, then?"

' "Oh, gracious me!" she laughed. "Don't you know? Oh, Blanche, you never notice anything! Harry's in love with her."

'I caught my breath and put my hands in my lap so that she should not see them tremble. "Lucy, don't you know that's a very vulgar way to talk? And stupid too."

' "But he is, he is. He writes poetry. I've seen it. There's one about when she kisses him good-bye every morning," she said, her eyes sparkling with mischief.

'But I was not amused. "Faugh!" I exclaimed. "How unspeakably revolting!" I put my handkerchief to my lips.

' "Oh, Blanche, how stodgy you've got since you're married!" my sister complained. "Once you'd have seen how funny it is. Harry being grown-up and sighing and looking in the glass."

' "It isn't funny," I insisted. "It's terrible and disgusting and *wrong*. You're too young to understand. You must never mention it to anyone again. For if Papa heard about it he would punish Harry dreadfully."

'Her eyes were round as blue glass buttons.

' "What would Papa do to him?" she breathed.

' "He'd send him away for being so wicked."

' "Like – like Robert?" she whispered.

'I nodded. She looked quite pale. I was satisfied.

'I cannot pretend I was worried at not hearing from Sophia; I simply felt absolved from my obligations. Until I received a cable from Papa to the effect that Sophia had cabled news to him of her miscarriage and would I instantly cable details and report on her condition. Then I was horrified. Not only had I not known that Sophia had had a miscarriage, I did not even know where she was, and had not troubled to find out the nature of her illness. I was flooded with guilt. Not remorse; I was not sorry for her in the least, but I did feel horribly guilty at having failed Papa. And worse, I did not see my way to mend the situation. I did not know where she was, nor did I know the name of her doctor, and Oliver was not there to advise me. Yet plainly I could neither ignore Papa's cable nor cable him back the full extent of my ignorance.

'Then, like an angel visiting me in my despair, I recollected Mrs Falk, Sophia's neglected mother. I would go to her. She would be sure to know where her daughter was and would direct me to her.

'I had never been to London by myself and because I did not know that part of London I took a four-wheeler to her address. I sat on the edge of the seat nervously glancing through my veil at the dizzying traffic and holding stiffly away from me the bouquet of pink carnations I was bringing for Sophia.

'As we turned into the street where Mrs Falk lodged, I saw on the other side of the road a woman very like Sophia in just such a walking-dress as she had in lavender broadcloth frogged with violet braid, but her face was concealed beneath a pale grey silk parasol and she passed too briskly for me to be certain of her walk, for all my craning to see through the dusty little window behind. Of course I knew very well it could not be she; only it was queer to chance on someone so like her in this very street.

'The street had come down in the world, the residences were no longer so genteel and shops were beginning to creep in at either end, as if they did not like to establish themselves boldly in the centre among the fanlights that offered discreet little notices: "Apartments to let". The cabby drew up

before an old-fashioned house built in the days when the
Italian style was in vogue and it was still embellished with
the useless little ornamental ironwork balconies, now sadly
faded and forlorn. The worn stone stairs rang under my
feet. They circled up into the gloom. Mrs Falk's apartments
were on the third floor. It was a very long time before
anyone answered the door and then it was opened three
inches and a crone put one eye to the gap and demanded to
know who it was. I said I wanted to see Mrs Falk.

' "Who is that?" she repeated sharply.

'I said my name was Mrs Bridgewater. Whereupon the
creature snapped, "Not at home!" and slammed the door in
my face. I rang again and waited. I rang repeatedly. For it
occurred to me that the servant might know Sophia's
address, and since it was my only hope I determined not to
leave without discovering it. At last I heard the chain
rattling on the door and it was opened once more.

' "Whatyer want?" the creature asked surlily.

' "I wondered if you could give me Mrs Sheridan's present address?"

'Sallow, squat as a toad, she eyed me with an opaque
reptilian stare that I found extremely offensive. Despite
myself, I stared back fascinated.

' "Better come in," she said, turning and waddling away,
leaving me to follow. She shuffled along in heelless red slippers, and it was only then that I noticed that she was
dressed in an absurd trailing wrap of shoddy pink tinsel
edged with some ragged brown fur and I realised that she
was not the servant, but Sophia's mother.

'She led me into a crowded stuffy parlour that smelt of
dust, as though the windows had not been opened since
time began. She humped herself into a buttoned armchair,
her short legs dangling like a child's, and placed a wrinkled
yellow hand glittering with jewels on each thigh. Her scanty
locks dyed a dark red were carefully varnished in curls
across her bald skull. I decided that it was the way her head
was folded into her shoulders that gave her her obscenely

reptilian appearance. She was an object of pure horror. It was impossible to imagine that anyone had loved this creature and married her, and that from her womb had sprung the beautiful Sophia.

' "Well?" she cried impatiently, thrusting out her square jaw. "Whatyer want now yer here?"

' "I should like to see Sophia. I am anxious to know how she is; particularly so, as my father – "

' "What makes you think she's here?" she interrupted me harshly.

' "I don't, of course," I said politely. "Only I hoped you would be able to give me her address. She – it was all so sudden, she left without – and now I suppose is too ill to write. It is so sad," I added conventionally, watching the wrinkled claws pridefully smoothing the soiled pink gauze over her thighs.

' "Those flowers for her? You can leave 'em here. I'll see she gets 'em."

' "Thank you. I'd rather give them to her myself. I've come to London specially. If you could give me her address I need not trouble you – "

' "No," she said. "I can't."

' "You mean you don't know it either?" I asked in alarm.

' "What I do know I know enough to keep to meself," she observed sardonically.

'I felt stupefied by this delphic manner. She had not asked me to sit down and now I asked if I might. I sat on a spindly Regency chair that creaked under me. I laid the carnations on the curio-table.

' "Then you know but you won't tell me," I said incredulously. "It isn't for myself I want to know, it's for P – it's for Mr Sheridan. He's very worried . . . so far away, you see."

'When she silently laughed like that all the brooches and ear-rings and ornaments with which she was bedizened flashed brilliantly alive in their dirty gold settings. It occurred to me that the old woman might be a little mad.

' "She'll be back. Tell yer Pappy she'll be back. Sophie's

always been a sensible gal," she assured me grotesquely with her wide toad's mouth a-grin.

'I felt stifled and afraid. I had never fainted in my life, but I had the absurd notion that I was going to faint now. I pressed my wrist to my brow and rose up shakily to beg a glass of water.

' "*I've* no maid, my fine young lady," she announced, feeling for the floor with her short legs, her paws rasping on the satin arms of the chair.

' "Pray don't trouble," I muttered, fumbling my way past the little dark objects that seemed to have placed themselves between me and the door. "I'll find my way."

'I stood in the dingy hall wondering which of the four doors facing me concealed the kitchen. Well, I should not find out by standing there! I opened the nearest door: a long narrow window dimly lit an unmade bed hung with stained green curtains, in the middle of whose tumbled sheets a dark object lay like a muff – a small stertorous dog; there was a tray of food by the bed; the dressing-table shone white with dust; clothes lay wrinkled on the floor; the night-commode stood ajar. I caught a glimpse of myself in the mirror opposite, startled, white-faced, and withdrew hurriedly.

'The next room was as bright and neat as the other was foul, yet what I saw there made me bolt out again faster than I entered – as if I had inadvertently intruded on someone undressing. Indeed the shock was much the same. The vase of mauve carnations made me feel that Sophia was actually there, discovered in her nakedness, though the room was empty. But that startled glimpse had not been too brief for me to catch sight of Oliver's red silk robe flung over the back of a chair by the bedside and underneath it, primly matched, the embroidered gondolier's slippers I had bought him in Venice as a souvenir. My heart was beating so painfully that I was forced to cling to the door handle for support.

'I was in terror that old Mrs Falk would come out and

find me there. For I understood only too plainly now why she could not give me her daughter's address. I do not say that I grasped the whole plot at once. At that moment I only knew that Sophia and Oliver were living in that room together. It was later than I understood the miscarriage was a fiction; there never had been a baby, it was simply a device to absent herself from Papa's company and remain with Oliver while her husband was conveniently away. I remembered innumerable little details which before had seemed odd and incomprehensible, but were now suddenly plain.

'I could have run away then, but I dared not leave without my flowers. So I returned to the airless parlour where old Mrs Falk sat with her toes stretched out before her, admiring her feet with a thoughtful grin.

'I said, "I would rather you did not tell your daughter about my visit, Mrs Falk. She will doubtless write to me as soon as she is able; it would be better to leave it till then."

' "Changed yer mind, have yer? Second thoughts best, eh?" she chuckled. "I somehow fancied yer might. So now it's to be a secret between you and me, eh? Something yer don't even want yer hubby to know," she leered with her loose-lipped grin.

' "Like the toad, ugly and venomous," I kept thinking, "ugly and venomous . . . " I could not remember the rest. I wondered if she knew what I had seen and the idea turned me cold inside; it put me so at her mercy, and I could hardly suppose she was to be trusted. Nor indeed was there any reason why she should be loyal to me. Her loyalty must be all for her daughter, whose treachery she approved.

'She heaved herself round in her chair and got down. I tried to say good-bye and picked up my flowers casually, but she ignored me and waddled into the hall trailing her tattered gown and I followed after. There she cautiously unbarred the door, peered about her and then closed it again.

' "Listen," she said, bringing her evil old face uncomfortably close to mine. "A word of advice for those who can take it. Never try and get the better of Sophia. You won't succeed. I should know. Yes, I should know," she muttered. "I could tell you things," she went on, her treacly black eyes fastened on mine. And then as abruptly she changed her mind and, much to my relief, let go my arm, to whine in her high harsh voice, "But no one wants to hear what a poor mad old woman has to tell. Bundle her under ground and stamp on her! Ugh, nasty old creature! Eh?"

'But her eyes were not mad, they were sly and watchful and they frightened me. I said quickly, "Well, good-bye, Mrs Falk, and thank you awfully," as cheerfully as I could, and made my escape.'

CHAPTER SIX

DEATH IN THE AFTERNOON

Alva Hine fell into an abstraction, which the young man respected for a while and then with a certain subdued impatience enquired what she had done then.

'Oh, I went home again, and waited for my husband and my stepmother to return in their own good time.' She made a small hopeless gesture. 'What else was there to do?'

'Couldn't you have divorced him?' he asked with all the simplicity of ignorance.

'Oh, my dear sir,' she exclaimed, shocked. 'You have no idea what you are saying! Divorce was unheard of in those days. Such a thing would never have occurred to me. Besides, mere adultery was not sufficient reason in law for a divorce; there had to be cruelty and desertion as well. They had at all costs,' she said with carefully mild irony, 'to preserve the sanctity of marriage.'

'My God!' ejaculated Mr Jones disgustedly. 'Yet . . . still . . . surely,' he hesitated. 'You could have left him?' he suggested.

'Mr Jones! Mr Jones! You speak of what you do not understand. In theory I could have left him, yes. But, gone where? Lived on what money? How earned my bread? Oh, we were well trapped in those days; ignorant, untrained, frivolous, and hobbled with conventions. I had not even Sophia's aptitude for dainty little water-colours. Oh, no, I could not escape, believe me, or I would have done! I did my best to escape *with* Oliver, to persuade him to find a small house somewhere where we could be alone together, as married people should, and far, far, from Sophia. But of course he would not. Indeed, to be just, he could not, since he was entirely dependent on Papa; and though I wrote to *him* begging him to allow us to move into a place of our own, he wrote back curtly that it was out of the question and pretended he could not afford it. Oh, I admit it, I was in despair all those weeks. And then to my dismay I found myself with child. A man can never know what it means to bear an unwanted child, within one's own body, to be ever conscious with horror and dread of this growing burden inescapably lodged in one's flesh. Yes, that is not pleasant,' said Miss Hine more mildly, as if agreeing with herself.

'I began to notice about this time that Harry was looking drawn and unhappy. He used to sit silent over dinner averting his eyes from Sophia and directly the meal was over would leave the room. And since I too could no longer endure to contribute to this artificial situation, I would soon make my excuses to retire. Thus, Sophia and my husband were left for long agreeable hours together. Let us compute quite baldly; they could enjoy their uninterrupted society from, say, eight-thirty p.m. till they parted for the night at about eleven. Because I hated and feared them both and saw no way out of my horrible predicament, I tried not to think about them, tried to escape from them in my mind because I might not escape physically, tried dully not to consider their doings.

'Harry and I became nearer to one another again, as we were in childhood. He was kind to me and gentle. He demanded nothing from me and never spoke to me about his troubles. Simply I suppose the continuity of our affection comforted us a little. In this half-silent companionship we would walk across the flats, leaving a pattern of footprints in the brown sand, skirting the shallow pools filled with evening gold.

'The days shortened. August was hot that year, hot and grey and broken with thunderstorms. Sophia seemed to find it exceptionally trying. She trailed about the house, heavy-eyed, the beautiful china-white bloom of her skin become waxen, or wandered into the unfrequented parts of the garden, lifting tendrils of green shade out of her path, fronds of bracken brushing her skirts. Beyond the kitchen garden was a small wilderness that she made her own. There tall grasses swept her knees and swags of Dorothy Perkins showered down from the heart of an ancient pear tree. She would sit dull-struck for hours on a stone bench there, with a book on her knee, staring at the iris blades rosetted with snails.

'I wondered if she were falling out of love with Oliver? Or, more likely, if he had fallen out of love with her? That would best account for her look of weariness and hidden anxiety, would explain her vanished gaiety, her vanished prettiness that somehow – however much one hated her one could not deny – turned all to grace. She became careless in her dress, more matronly, less fastidious. I heard her once in a fit of sobbing inside her room, and I wondered if it was exultation or pity that made my heart beat so fiercely. And when she came down afterwards she looked bloated and obese, like some swollen drowned thing, and I had a sudden horrifying vision of her when she was old; immensely fat, white as turnips or candlewax, and coarse as only red-haired people can coarsen.

'No more tea-parties now, no more village fêtes; she seemed to shun being seen. When she went abroad now it was always in the carriage. She would drive to Ipswich or Colchester. Thomas said it was to make purchases at the chemist. But if so, she was very secretive about it. Sometimes she would descend from the carriage and walk down one or two turnings to the chemist she wanted, but whether that was in the attempt to deceive the coachman or the chemist it would be hard to say. Anyway, Thomas used to jig up his horse and follow at a distance. I think Thomas did not approve of ladies going on secret errands, or maybe he merely considered it his duty to protect her.

'Sophia would come back with her bottles and pills, but if they were to brighten her complexion, they did not prove of much use, and a week later the carriage would be ordered again.

'Yes, it is easy to see now that I was very naïve, very gullible, but I truly had no suspicion of what was up. It was not in fact until I had Papa's cable from Marseilles to say that he was on his way home unexpectedly early (he had been gone barely seven months), would be arriving on the following Tuesday, wanted it to be a surprise for Sophia, but thought he had better let me know. Of course it was not possible to keep it from her. She had to know. Oliver and Harry had already left for Town when I told her.

'She listened to my news quite blankly with a pre-occupied expression as if all her attention was taken up with something more inwardly important, except that her skin took on a curious sickly-green tinge and she threw up her hands as though to ward off the blackness which descended on her like a great cloak flung over her head. She lay tumbled on the floor. I found her smelling-salts and put them to her nose.

' "It was the heat," she said, looking up at me with eyes from which all the colour seemed to have fled. "What were you saying?"

' "Before you fainted? Why, only that Papa would be back on Tuesday. But that surely could not have upset you."

' "Of course not," she said. "It was the heat. I – help me up, Blanche, please."

' "I think you should lie still awhile."

' "I shall be all right now. Such good news will revive me wonderfully," she said with a pale smile. "The prospect of seeing Edward again so soon is almost more than I can take in."

' "Papa means it for a surprise. You are not supposed to know anything about it," I warned her. "You will have to simulate great astonishment; shall you know how to pretend to something you do not feel?" I asked disingenuously.

'But when I ventured to glance at her from the corner of

my eyes to see how she had swallowed that remark, I was shocked to see how haggard she looked.

' "A surprise?" she muttered drily. "Why, what does he expect to find?" she said and put her hand to her heart.'

'I said sharply, "I said you should lie still awhile. You're ashen." But she would not listen to me and presently I went away.

'It was later that day, that evening to be precise, that I learnt more. I greeted Oliver punctiliously on his return as always (I suppose because women always try to hide the verities of their private life from their domestics), and on this occasion as I turned away I chanced to glance at myself in the big gilt mirror but my eye was taken instead by my stepmother in the doorway looking, as it were, beyond the mirror to where Oliver stood. She was only there an instant, but her look was agitated and intense and I distinctly saw her say: "I must see you alone," before she vanished. I cannot think why this should have made me especially watchful. They constantly did see one another alone and I thought nothing of it. But it was her low spirits and agitation that impressed me with the significance of this occasion. It was so obvious that something was wrong, and was I mistaken in connecting it with Papa's return, or was it only that I wanted everything to be right this time when he came back?

'At all events she did not get a moment alone with him before dinner. So that when I "remembered" to tell Oliver the news of Papa it came as much a surprise to him as it had to Sophia.

' "Good God!" he exclaimed, shocked out of his habitual composure, and he could not prevent a hasty glance at Sophia's bent enigmatic face.

'I smiled. "Isn't it splendid?" I said.

' "Splendid," he concurred, and thereafter fell silent.

'Harry as usual went up early but I sat grimly on with my sewing watching them. Oliver was hidden behind the paper but Sophia was miserably restless. At last she sat at the piano and began playing Liszt with a confusion of noise that betrayed a desperation that was half-insane it seemed to me. At last I yawned and said I should take a turn in the garden before bed.

'I stood in the dark garden listening to their voices.

' "What are we to do, Noll?" said Sophia in a low anguished voice. "What are we to do?"

' "It was so unexpected; I've had no time to consider."

' "You *must* think of something!" she commanded in her old way.

' "There's still the midwife."

' "When only last month a girl died under her filthy ministrations? Yes, I suppose it would solve the problem quite neatly for you if I died," she said bitterly.

' "Don't be so absurd," he admonished her lightly. "You gruesome little thing!"

' "Besides, it's too late for that. Much too late."

' "Then, what?" he asked. "Should we clear out together?"

' "What would be the use of that?" she exclaimed angrily. "The ruination of all we've worked for; the waste of all these years. How can you be so frivolous at a moment like this? Consider the scandal, it would mean the ruin of your career! We should be penniless, worse off than we are now, and on top of all that, a child – to ruin my good name. Oh, ruin, ruin, ruin, whichever way I turn! What is to be done?"

' "I give up," he announced like a child unable to solve a riddle.

' "My dear Oliver, you are in this just as much as I am; it is useless for you to fold your hands and say you can do no more."

' "Tell me what I am to do and I will do it."

' "Oh, I am so wretched! I have dosed myself sick, and all my courage is gone. I am afraid of Edward. He is beyond reason in his passion for me. This will kill him."

' "Perhaps that is the solution," he said.

' "What do you mean?"

' "If he should die . . . " he said lightly.

'I stood there numb as a stone. I could feel the stored warmth of the bricks on my cold flesh as I leaned against the wall in a chill of horror. Thoughts buzzed in my head like furious bees. Above me the stars pricked their spears through the floor of heaven. I wanted to hide from their sight and in a blind movement stumbled into the haven of dark trees. I did not know that I was weeping till I put my hands to my face and found my cheeks were wet.'

'Had you not realised that your stepmother was pregnant before that?' asked Lancelot Jones.

'I was a very stupid young woman,' confessed old Miss Hine. 'I should think you had realised that by now. But although that was an indubitable shock, it was not why I wept. My grief was for Papa. I was in a positive terror for him. I believed with Sophia that the discovery would kill him, or break his heart and crush him so utterly that he would be happier dead.

'How long I wandered in the warm, moth-frequented garden I do not know, but eventually I was found there by Harry and in my rage and impotence and terror I blurted out all the truth to him. It was unforgivable of me of course; but we had grown so much closer in these last weeks, and besides I had my reasons – I needed him as a supplementary witness. Poor child, he was overwhelmed! Sophia had awakened in him all the first intensity of adolescent love. He worshipped her. To him she was the Mother-Goddess. And then she became bored with his adoration and pretty boyish ways, or more simply had no further use for him once Papa had gone away. In his innocent wretchedness he could not understand her icy indifference. He confessed all this to me as we wandered in the mild September night or sat within the close darkness of the cedar we had so often climbed.' The old woman shrugged with bland philosophy, 'Ah, well! we are all heirs to these shocks in our very nature so the sooner we accustom ourselves to the legacy the better, I suppose. I told myself Harry would get over it. We all had to.

'At all events, everybody contrived to put on a good show for Papa when he returned. We cooed and petted and patted the "returned hero" while Harry and Oliver assumed appropriately awkward attitudes – men being so much less apt at dissimulation. Only little Edgar was unperturbed and unselfconscious – not quite remembering Papa but welcoming the new face without gush.

'I suppose we all felt a little unfamiliar with Father, so much had happened since he went away that he felt quite a stranger to us. There was one uncomfortable moment when he produced the presents he had brought for us all, and among them a girdle for Sophia of filigree gold gemmed with turquoise, a beautiful example of Singhalese metal-work, but alas embarrassingly too small for Sophia's enlarged waist. A betraying tide of crimson dyed her throat. But when he wanted her to put it on she went deathly white and pushed it from her.

' "I'm sorry," she said, "you could not know, Edward, but turquoise are fatally unlucky to me. I never wear them."

' "Come, my dearest, how absurdly fanciful! This is most unlike you! We are not barbarians, I hope, to believe that stones and stars and colours can influence our lives."

' "Yes, but I do believe that, Edward," she said in a shaking voice.

' "No, no, no," he laughed. "Was there ever such a silly little woman before! Come, precious, just try it! To please me! I'll vouch for it you won't drop dead," he teased.

' "Don't make me, Edward, please!"

' "My dear, how strange you are!" he observed in dismay. "What can be the matter that a pretty woman should refuse to wear something so elegant *and*, by the way, costly?"

' "I'm not ungrateful, Ned dear," she said, coming to him prettily, "but humour my whim for the present, will you? I daresay it is just a fancy of mine and I am a very foolish little person, but – "

'I could tell from the way he looked at her that he was as

much under her dominion as ever. They appeared oblivious
of anyone else in the room, Papa lost in her eyes. I said, "In
any case, Papa, it is much too small for Sophia. You'll have
to give it to Lucy."

'Lucy clapped with delight. And Papa said, "My dear, I
know the size of my wife's trim little waist," and he slipped
an arm about her as she stood close.

' "Alas," she said lightly with great composure, "I am no
longer the girl I was, since you went away, Ned. I never
regained my figure after my illness. You left a girl, you've
come back to a woman," she said, giving him a long look.
And the difficult moment passed away.

'I wondered for how long Sophia would be able to keep
her secret now that Papa was home. She was tight-lacing
excessively at this time and twice she fainted. It would
appear that the remedy might prove riskier than the com-
plaint. How did Sophia hope to resolve this hopeless situation, which clearly could not last much longer without
something giving under the strain, I wondered. I found
myself watching her uneasily. Watching Papa. Watching
Oliver. I could not get out of my head the tone in which
Oliver had said, "Perhaps that is the solution," and "If he
should die!" It was like a teasing echo in my brain. Once
when Oliver himself poured a glass of wine for Papa and
brought it to him, I took care to spill it with deliberate
clumsiness.'

'Why?' interpolated the young man at this point.

The old woman blinked at him.

'I was afraid,' she said simply. 'I was afraid they were
planning to murder him. It was more than just hysteria, you
know; there really was a sense of evil about the place, palp-
able, heavy and unbearably cloying – one could not seem to
shake it off.

'And then on Friday, the 13th of September, the Friday
after Papa's homecoming, the situation abruptly ended.

'It was a day of oppressive heat, and nerves were taut and
tempers short. Harry and Oliver had gone to Town as

usual, but Papa (though he had gone up to London on the
Wednesday and Thursday) had much business to attend to
at home, he said, and had remained closeted in his room,
writing, all day. Lucy and I had taken a picnic-tea on the
dunes with Edgar – a thing we had not done for many a day.
We were back before six because of Edgar's bed-time. Papa
stood morosely in the hall with his letters for the post in his
hand and enquired where Sophia was.

'I said I supposed in the garden, if she was not in the
house. I heard him calling her as he went . . . I climbed the
stairs wearily to take off my straw bonnet with the pansies. I
felt suddenly so tired I could have cried. But I thought of
Papa, and after I had washed my hands and combed my
hair smooth, I went down to look for him.

'I found him with Sophia in the little wild garden. He did
not see me or hear me approach. He had caught hold of a
bramble that would otherwise have struck his face, and was
gripping it, unconscious of the thorns driving into his flesh.
He was staring at her where she sat, or rather lay, half-
tumbled off the curved stone bench, her red unloosened
hair blazing in the last low gleams of sunlight, like strands of
fire against the dark cascade of ivy buzzing with metallic
flies. They were the only sound in that still garden. Her
collar had burst open with the violence of her movement,
and her skirt fell in a lovely sculptured movement from her
parted knees. She reminded me, among the briars and
convolvulus and glistening webs, of Ophelia. One could
have thought she had but fainted until one saw her face.
One could not have imagined so hideous a terror, such an
inhuman convulsion. I gave a cry when I saw it which
roused Papa from his stupor.

'He looked at me with great blank eyes.

' "What has happened?" he said, in a hoarse yet muted
voice.

'I went to him. I put my face on his breast. I said, "Oh,
Papa! My poor Papa! Come away! She's *dead*!" ' '

CHAPTER SEVEN

MR PIERCE ENQUIRES

'I rang for Beulah as soon as we got back to the house and told her to run for the doctor, Mrs Sheridan had been taken ill. Papa looked pallid, drenched, and dazed as if he had been hit across the eyes. I poured him a stiffish brandy to pull him together before the doctor arrived. I suppose it was his necessity that kept me from collapse.

'The doctor was new to us. I do not suppose a doctor had been in the house since Mama died. People coddled themselves less then, and we were always a healthy family. Dr Scott proved to be one of those hearty, florid types whose bedside manner consists of the genial conviction that all illness is nonsense. "Well, well, well," he exclaimed bluffly, rubbing his hands with simple pleasure at the prospect of a new and wealthy patient. "What's the trouble?" I wondered how he would deal with "the trouble", but he had another face for death. He became professional in a different way.

'I fancied that he touched the dead woman more gently than he would the living. It did not take him long, after all, to find out that life was quite extinct. Papa asked in a queer high voice how she had died.

' "There will have to be an autopsy to determine the cause of death," said Dr Scott.

' "No," said Papa. "I won't have that. Let her alone! What good will it do now? What does it matter why she died? My dear one has suffered enough," he said in this high unnatural voice, and then grotesquely began to sob.

' "I'm afraid there is no alternative," said the doctor stiffly. "I cannot sign the Death Certificate until the cause of death is determined. In a case of sudden and unnatural death like this I am sure you will understand that, however unpleasant it may seem, it is my duty to send for the police."

'Papa echoed, "The police?" in a stunned voice.

'I felt a sudden nausea. There was a fly, a little buzzing glittering fly, walking up and down the white unbroken line of Sophia's throat and this tiny irrelevant detail made me realise as nothing else had that Sophia was irrevocably dead. The black buzzing insect grew larger and louder to my senses till I was swallowed up in the noisy blackness.

'There was the bitter scent of crushed ivy in my nostrils when I came to myself and my eyes opened on to its dull black berries and stiff glossy leaves, like a funeral wreath at my head, where I had pitched down. The doctor would not let me be there when the police came, he said I must be careful in my condition, I had already been put under excessive strain. He said Papa must look after me. And I was glad of the excuse to get Papa away from there. Papa sat by my couch and stroked my hand sadly with a guilty expression. I felt very light and somehow not quite real. I could not understand why he looked so wretched, couldn't he understand that we should all be much happier without her?

'But that was where I was wrong. What is past is past and one can never go back, it was foolish of me to suppose things could ever be the same again.

'The police were still at their grim business in the garden when I heard our carriage wheels approaching with Oliver and Harry. I went to them at once to spare them the worst shock of brutal discovery. I suppose I must have been pale and wild-eyed, for Harry immediately sprang from the carriage and called, "What is the matter, Blanche Rose?"

' "It's all right," I said. "Don't be afraid!" And before I could get back my breath, Oliver said sharply:

' "Something's happened to Sophie! Hasn't it? Where is she? Let me go to her!" he said with something like a scream.

' "Oliver, you can't," I said, catching at his coat. He tore himself from me savagely, and began to run towards the house. I cried, "Harry, stop him! Oliver, you must take hold of yourself; you can't do anything now."

'He turned and stared at me.

' "She's dead," he muttered, white to the lips. "I knew it all the time." His blazing eyes met mine unseeingly with a tortured, accusing look.

'Harry said, "My poor Blanche! When did it happen?"

'I put my hand to my forehead. "We found her – I can hardly believe it – about an hour ago. The doctor and the police are still with her."

' "*The police?*" they cried together. "Why are the police here?"

' "They say it is a formality in cases of sudden death. You see, she was alone when she died," I explained gravely, "in the little garden – so no one knows yet how it happened."

'I did not want Oliver to see her, I did not want him to be haunted by the distorted horror of her face, but he would not be prevented. I walked between them across the lawns and through the weather-stained blue gate in the wall. Their immensely elongated shadows stalked before them in top hats as tall as chimney-pots, like a parody of mutes at a funeral.

'In their black City clothes they looked as grotesque in those natural surroundings as did the policemen. Someone had covered the dead woman's face. With a suppressed cry Oliver flung himself forward and dropped on his knees by the body. He would have thrown himself across her if a policeman had not seized hold of him. For a few moments they wrestled in silence with a rather sinister solemnity, and in doing so one of them brushed against the body and dislodged it a little so that a fold of the skirt was freed, and from it came fluttering a white butterfly and rested on the ground. It was only a piece of paper about two inches across by three. There did not appear to be anything written on it or any other marks, except that it had been creased twice in neat parallels across the length and the breadth. I could have told him what it was if he had asked me, but as soon as he caught sight of it the policeman loosed Oliver and picked it up, turning it in his fingers curiously before slipping it into an envelope. Only then did he turn to Oliver and say, "I'm sorry, sir, if I handled you a bit rough, but I must ask you not to interfere with the deceased until we have concluded our survey."

' "Oh, my God! *The deceased!*" said Oliver and began to laugh.

'The policeman shook him like a doll, I suppose because it was the only way to stop Oliver's hysteria. Oliver propped himself against a tree, limp exhausted, white as a pierrot.

' "May I have your name, sir?" said the policeman civilly with the appalling persistence of his kind.

'I went to Oliver and put my arm through his. He looked so fagged and lost that I answered for him. "He is my husband," I said in a high clear voice, "Mr Oliver Bridgewater. He was a cousin of the second Mrs Sheridan's," I said in explanation of his behaviour, for surely it is permissible to be shocked into hysteria at the sudden violent demise of a near relative. "The young gentleman is my brother," I added, indicating Harry who stood looking frightened a little way away.

' "I shall be obliged if the lady and gentlemen will leave us now to finish our business. I shall want to see you later," the policeman said.

' "What about?" I asked, turning back sharply at his last remark.

' "We'll take things as they come, if you don't mind, madam. You will learn what it is about when we arrive at that point," he said calmly. And from having been merely a public-serving nonentity like a waiter or a shop assistant, I saw him suddenly as an obstinate human being like myself with a dangerous dislikeable personality.

'As we returned to the house I told the two men as much as I knew myself about the tragedy. I said, "I can't think why that stupid policeman should want to talk to you when you were neither of you here."

' "Oh, they have to get everything ship-shape and correct," Harry said knowingly. "Don't worry, Blanche, dear, it won't be anything."

' "It couldn't be, dear, could it?" I said easily.

'It was fidgety waiting for the policeman, for he did not come at once; I had time to comb out my hair and wind it up again and bathe my hands in cologne water.

'Beulah tapped at the door and said that Mr Pierce was asking to see me.

' "Mr Pierce?" I said. "I can see no one now. Did he tell you his business?"

' "It's the policeman, M'm."

'It amused me that he had given his name. I said, "Where is he?"

' "In the drawing-room," she said.

' "You should have put him in the morning-room, Beulah," I said sharply. This was altogether too much of a good thing. The man was presumptuous. "You should know by now that only expected visitors are shown to the drawing-room; callers are put in the morning-room; and *persons* are left in the hall. He could have waited in the hall."

' "I didn't put him nowhere, M'm; he just went."

' "Beulah, you are a very silly girl. Pray, what would you do if it had been a thief who *just went* to the drawing-room? You only had his word for it that he was a policeman, you know."

' "He was wearing 'is uniform, M'm."

' "Beulah, don't be pert! You may go," I said, looking at myself in the glass and tucking a clean handkerchief into my wristband. My serious, pale, young face gazed back at me, but I was pleased to note that I appeared cool and trim. I went slowly down.

'He was gazing at the portrait of Mama, looking very sweet and audacious in a blue sash with her fair hair frizzed out like Lucy's.

' "Ah," he said, turning to me. "The first Mrs Sheridan, and your mother, I presume, madam?" He shook his head. "I'm sorry to be obliged to intrude on your private grief at such a moment, but believe me, I have no choice in the matter. I can promise you not to keep you long. It is only to ask a few simple questions."

' "Won't you sit down?" I said. "What is it you want to know?"

' "In the first place, who last saw her alive?"

' "Gracious, I've no idea! Perhaps I did."

' "What time was that, madam?"

' "I'm afraid I never noticed. After luncheon, when she went upstairs to her room and I went down to see Cook about the picnic we were going on. Two o'clock or a little after, I suppose."

' "I see. And it was about six o'clock when she was found. Did she usually sit in that secluded corner? Was it a favourite nook of hers?"

' "Yes, she had taken rather a fancy to it, she liked to sit there alone."

' "And what frame of mind would you judge the deceased lady to have been in latterly?"

' "The same as usual, I think," I said cautiously.

' "Not in low spirits?"

'This seemed to me a little near the knuckle. I shook my head.

' "You would say, not worried?"

' "I don't see what she could have had to worry about."

' "She was apparently quite happy?" '

' "Why shouldn't she be, with her husband just returned?" I parried.

' "Oh? Has Mr Sheridan been away?" he said.

'I could have slapped myself for my carelessness! That's what came from trying to be too clever. Then I was obliged

to tell him that Father had been away in India and Ceylon
for half a year and had only returned on Tuesday.

'The policeman looked at me curiously.

' "Mr Sheridan did not mention any of this to me."

' "Perhaps he did not think it relevant," I suggested
lamely.

' "Not relevant, when his lady dies mysteriously and suddenly directly he comes back?"

' "But – but – " I stammered, "what could his return
have to do with it? Her death was an accident . . . Wasn't
it? – Wasn't it?" I repeated.

' "That will be for the Coroner to decide at the inquest,"
he said, quite placidly.

' "The inquest?" I whispered, staring. "Why must there
be an inquest?"

' "To discover how and why the deceased person met her
death."

' "But that's horrible, horrible!" I muttered, squeezing
my hands together. My face burned at the thought of the
scandal. Was there no way of stopping it, I begged? If I
lost my composure, it was at the sudden realisation that
Papa would learn, and in the most horrible way possible,
under the avid gaze of the public, of his dead wife's infidelity.

'The policeman hastened to assure me that it would all be
quite straightforward, nothing to worry about.

' "It won't seem like nothing, madam, to a young lady
with your presence of mind," he said. "Really remarkable
how you took a hold of yourself straight after coming upon
your dead stepmother like that. I wouldn't care for a
daughter of mine to see such a shocking sight. And it being,
in a manner of speaking, a near relative, makes it worse of
course." He gave me a birdlike glance and added: "People
laugh at the idea of having women in the police force, but I
fancy that if we could count on ladies like you we might find
it very advantageous." '

Mr Jones was frowning in his corner.

'Did you really imagine Sophia had died by accident?' he asked.

Miss Hine gave him a long considering stare, and at last, choosing her words with care, said:

'It was what I wanted to think.'

CHAPTER EIGHT

FROM 'THE KILL' TO 'A VIEW'

'The inquest was held on Saturday afternoon in the village schoolroom with its wooden forms and deal desks grained and varnished a hideous yellow to imitate oak. The place smelt of hot varnish and dust,' said Miss Hine reminiscently.

'After the jurymen had viewed the body, the Coroner began calling the witnesses. Beulah was the first, her smug little suety face, finished off with a tight round buttonhole of a mouth, shiny with importance under a toque apparently constructed from glistening black Pontefract Cakes.

'She said the last time she had seen her mistress was when she was airing the rooms, as was the custom, for ten minutes or so in the middle of the day if it was fine. As she crossed the hall she had seen Mrs Sheridan come downstairs and go out into the garden and across the lawn to where she always sat to take the air. That would have been about three o'clock, as near as she could say.

' "Did she speak to you?" asked the Coroner.

' "She didn't see me."

' "Did you see her alive again?"

' "Naow," said Beulah with her pretty Essex accent.

' "Then we may assume that you were the last person known to have seen her alive?"

' "Naow," said Beulah, enjoying herself primly.

' "Who saw her after that?"

' "The young man must'uv."

' "What young man?"

' "I don't know 'is nime."

' "Where did you see him?"

' " 'E come to the 'ouse. 'E said 'e wanted to see the

Master, but when I arst for 'is nime 'e wooden' give it. 'E was saucy. When I tole 'im the Master wooden' see hanyone without they give their nime 'e wrote somethin' daown on a bitter piper and put it hinside a honvelope for me to tike to 'im. But the Master wooden' see 'im even then. 'E was ever so put out."

' "Who was, the young man?"

' "Naow, the Master. 'E tore the piper up ever so small an' looked proper upset. The young man looked real wild when I tole 'im, sour enough to turn the milk. Ooh, I thought, I wooden' like to get the wrong side of *yew*!"

' "What happened then?"

' " 'E arst to see Mrs Sheridan. I said she was in the garden, but before I 'ad time to go an' arse if she would see 'im, 'e said not to bother, 'e'd fine 'er 'imself, an' 'e run off before I 'ad a chance to do a thing."

' "What did you do then?"

' "Went inside and shut the door."

'Papa was called next and was asked about the mysterious young man. He said it was not anyone he knew, nor anyone he wished to see, and the name meant nothing to him. While he was away a lot of business had accumulated for him to attend to, which was why he had spent yesterday in his study and except for luncheon had not come out until the late afternoon when his letters were ready for the post. He had gone then to look for his wife. He described finding her in the garden, in bald uninflected sentences, struggling the while to keep his composure. Which indeed he almost lost when the Coroner asked him if he and his wife were on good terms.

' "The best of terms," he said, looking very white.

' "I believe you have been abroad?"

' "Yes. For seven months," said Papa.

'After that I was questioned, but I was only expected to confirm Papa's testimony, and describe how I had spent my day. Then came a plump good-natured young woman, like a farmer's daughter, with nice red cheeks and golden curls more natural than nature, and an absurdly magnificent hat.

' "What is your name?" said the Coroner.

' "Law!" she said good-humouredly. "You know me. I'm Polly Snoakes, barmaid at The Shepperton Horse."

'The Shepperton Horse was the only hostelry in the village. I could not imagine what she could possibly have to do with Sophia's death, but it was about the mysterious "caller" that she was asked to tell. It appears that he had arrived at The Shepperton Horse on the Thursday evening, saying he wanted to stay for a couple of nights. He gave his name as Dunstable. He spent most of his time in the saloon talking about Canada or asking questions about the village and in particular the people who lived at The Grange, but was inclined to be archly mysterious about himself. Polly Snoakes took him for a "commercial". Friday afternoon he came downstairs looking quite spruced-up and told her he was going to try his luck. She never saw him again. And though he "skipped" without paying for his lodging, he must have come back to the inn because his traps were gone.

'Strangers were so rare in our village that there was not much doubt about it being the same person as the one who had called at our house on the afternoon in question. I could not but think it odd. I stole a glance at Papa but his face was carefully expressionless.

'The next witness of importance was Dr Scott who declared he had performed the autopsy on the deceased. I was surprised to hear him describe her as a woman about thirty years old, for we had none of us doubted it when she said she was twenty-four. Once I should have been scornful to have found her in a lie, now it only seemed rather pathetic.

'Dr Scott said:

' "The deceased was in a normally healthy condition of pregnancy, at the beginning of the fourth month."

'I dared not look at Papa. I did not need to. I had secretly taken his hand in mine between the chairs, and at these words of the doctor's it had suddenly become slippery with sweat. The hot schoolroom rustled horribly with whispers.

'The Coroner coughed uneasily.

' "Is this relevant, doctor?"

' "That is for you to judge, sir, I can merely report on my findings at the examination."

' "We are here to learn how the deceased met her death and any facts that strictly bear on the matter are naturally necessary to the verdict. You must not waste the time of the Court with irrelevant private matters nor pain the deceased's family with idle slanders. If it is relevant we must hear it, however unpleasant."

' "The deceased died of cyanide poisoning," said the doctor tartly. "Perhaps you will be good enough to tell me what facts are relevant to that."

'The Coroner directed him to continue.'

' "Death," said Dr Scott, "would have been instantaneous. And had taken place within one to three hours before I was sent for, for *rigor mortis* had not set in. Cyanide of potassium is the crystalline form of prussic acid and is a deadly poison."

'One of the jurymen asked if it would be possible to take it by mistake for something else.

' "I mean," he said, "could one use it in error for some other substance such as sugar, for example?"

' "If one were not paying attention to what one was doing and the poison was in some easily accessible place, it would not be beyond the bounds of possibility," the doctor conceded. "But cyanide of potassium is hardly the sort of thing one would keep in the store-cupboard or the larder."

' "Unless it were put there on purpose," muttered the juryman.

' "It would be as well to make it clear that it is by no means easy for the layman to procure. To obtain it from a retail chemist one must show good reason for requiring it, and one would also be obliged to sign the Poison Register," the doctor said firmly.

'Nothing else of great interest was brought out. They were clearly unable to determine whether the poison was self-administered deliberately or by accident. And if by accident, how had it come to be in her possession?

'The Coroner therefore presently adjourned the inquest so that further enquiries could be made to discover how and by whom the poison was procured.

'The next few days were dreadful. I think they were the most uncomfortable days of my life. Papa shut himself away in his room and would see no one – no one at all. Trays were left untouched outside his door. If it had not been that he could be heard from time to time pacing the floor we should not have known if he was alive or dead.

'Occasionally visitors came to the door with piously doleful faces in shocking contrast with their avid eyes. Or if one of us ventured out for a breath of different air we could feel their faces watching us all along the street like sun-flowers. Otherwise there was nothing whatever to do but sit idly all day in the darkened rooms. At least we could claim the respect due to a house of mourning. Yet there was nothing to fill those empty interminable hours but the inevitable uncomfortable, repetitious wondering about the dead woman and what had happened and how it had happened and what was to happen next. It was horrible. And all the time policemen were coming in and out of the house informally on their own silent business. Or, casually entering a room, one would chance upon a policeman quietly turning over the contents of a cupboard or private drawer. You can have no idea of the invasions a violent death can inflict on one's personal life. And one has to bear it. It does not require much imagination to see how this ceaseless polite spying presses on the nerves. The most guiltless feel painfully exposed at having all their trivial precious little secrets laid naked to the gaze of a common stranger. And one dare not lose one's temper, one dare not be driven to a scream; one knows in advance how sickeningly their apologies for "inconveniencing" one disclose underneath their stolid determination to get on with the job.

'And then there was the questioning. A policeman would politely ask to be spared a few minutes of one's time (as though one could offer the excuse of having anything else to do with one's time!) and then ask two or three unimportant questions, the significance of which one desperately tried to understand.

'One was faced perpetually with the moral problem; to tell what one knew, or, on the other hand, to try and hide everything. For, after all, was anything to be gained by learning the truth? What truth had already been uncovered had only caused irreparable damage, what possible good could come from further disclosures?

'So, to begin with, I kept the key to Sophia's little private drawer (which I had myself locked before ever the policemen came to the house – less for fear of them than to protect Papa) where I knew she kept all the little boxes and bottles she brought back from her expeditions to the various chemists she visited. But I could not hope to keep it secret for long. The police would not hesitate to force the little drawer or find a master key to fit it. Alternatively, if I removed the medicines I would need to be very sure of what I was about, for it would never do to produce them later if it should become necessary. Eventually I went to Mr Pierce and gave him the key which I said I had come across by chance in a little Battersea box.

'I said, "Could she not have procured the – that poison herself?"

' "With the intention of killing herself, you mean?" he asked.

' "Well, no, not exactly," I said. "I have heard that some-times people die by accident through taking too much of a medicine that has a dangerous amount of poison in it. It would be safe enough if no more than the prescribed dose were taken, but you know some people imagine that if they take twice as much medicine as they should, it will do them twice as much good. Isn't it possible that Mrs Sheridan in this way absorbed a deathly amount of the poison?"

'He made no answer, and after a moment I went on:

' "She had been taking a lot of medicine recently, I know. I don't know what it was or who prescribed for her, but I thought I should tell you that it was not anything she had made-up locally where she was known. That always struck me as a little strange. The coachman will tell you how he used to drive her to one of the nearby towns where she would often go from one chemist to another." I looked at him. "I thought perhaps one of these medicines might have contained some cyanide of potassium – isn't that what it's called?"

'Still he said nothing. He must have been in a "study" for when next I spoke, he jumped and said:

' "Beg pardon, madam, I was thinking. What you say certainly requires investigation. We shall make enquiries at all the chemists in the district – not easy of course when the enquiry concerns the sale of forbidden nostrums, but we shall do our best. It will at any rate be simple enough to find out from the police analyst if cyanide is a constituent of any abortifacient."

'I did not understand.

' "Mrs Sheridan was trying to procure herself an abortion, wasn't she?" He looked at me, and, raising his eyebrows, added very slowly and clearly as to a deaf imbecile: "She was trying to get rid of her unwanted child."

'I blushed, at a loss what to say; such subjects were strictly unmentionable still at that period. To have heard it from another woman's lips – say, Sophia's – would have been embarrassing enough, but for it to be uttered by someone of the opposite sex and a complete stranger at that! It is hardly to be wondered at that words failed me.

'I could feel him watching me.

' "If you didn't know, madam, I wonder what you

thought all these secret medicines were for? You know – "
he hesitated, and with a sharp narrow glance at me continued: "if she was looking for something with which to
commit suicide, she did not need to go to all that trouble."
'I stared at my fingers spread against the green plush
tablecloth and waited.
' "Did you know that there was already enough cyanide
of potassium in the house to wipe out the entire household?"
' "How could I?" I said through stiff lips. I scrambled my
shaking fingers into my lap. "Who – where did you find it?"
I asked, for something to say that would weaken the force of
his stare.
' "In the cellar."
' "The cellar! Oh!" I said in relief. "That's . . . " I broke
off.
' "Your brother bought it about a month ago."
' "Oh, yes, of course," I said eagerly. "It's quite all right,
you know. It's what he uses in his photography."
' "Yes," said Mr Pierce forbiddingly, and added, "So
everyone understands."
'I said hurriedly:
' "You mean that Mrs Sheridan could have taken it from
there, if that was what she wanted?"
' "Anyone could."
' "It was locked," I said. "Harry always kept it locked."
' "A little deal cupboard that any key would open, that a
lady could unlock with one of her own hairpins. I take it you
all knew the contents of that little cupboard your brother
kept locked in his dark-room?"
'I hesitated.
' "Mrs Sheridan knew," I said. "Because, when she first
married Papa, she used to help Harry quite a lot with his
photography."
' "Indeed?" He sounded surprised. "Your brother was
on good terms with her then?"
'I stared.

' "Of course. Why shouldn't he be? They – they got on very well together."

' "It was your brother who told me they hated each other."

'I opened my mouth and then closed it again without saying anything. If that was the way Harry wanted it . . .

'What I had forgotten was Sophia's aunt, Mrs Livingstone, who lived in the neighbourhood, you may remember. I suppose somebody should have done something about her and seen to it that the news was tactfully broken to old Mrs Falk too. Yet no one had thought of it. With the head of the house immured in his chamber, the enterprise of the rest of us seemed to have flagged and dwindled. We had nothing to do and were fretted with restlessness, and yet we seemed caught in a web of lethargy, which I suppose was caused by the shock of this violent act in the middle of our lives.

'I was dreadfully ashamed when I saw them; old Mrs Falk and Mrs Livingstone, I mean. I was standing by the window, the venetian blinds were still drawn but "open" to let in a certain amount of light, and through the dusty slats I could see an appallingly decrepit hackney carriage rattle up the drive and draw up at the steps. It stood there, and nothing happened. As if it was empty. As if it had come to fetch one of us away, I thought, with a little shiver of fascination that people describe as someone walking over one's grave. And then the whole vehicle heeled over like a sailing-ship caught by the wind amidships, and there cautiously prodded out a weird old head that I recognised with a sinking heart.

'Out she stumped, the malevolent witch, and behind her came the little twittering figure of Mrs Livingstone. I uttered an exclamation of dismay to see them climbing the steps, old Mrs Falk as black as a crow, humping herself up each one with immense difficulty and pressing all her weight, I could see, on little Mrs Livingstone's shoulder.

'Oliver said languidly, "What is it?" and Lucy came, pushing against my arm to see: "Gracious!" she cried.

"What horrors! Whoever are they? Why, it's Mrs Livingstone!"

' "The other is Stepmama's mother," I said.

'Oliver sprang up, pale as a ghost.

' "What's the matter?" I exclaimed.

' "I can't see her! You must say I'm out. Please,
Blanche!"

' "And, pray, how am I to – " I began in protest, but at
that moment Beulah came in with Mrs Livingstone's card
on a salver.

' "They arse to see the Master, M'm, but I did say 'ow 'e
cooden' see anyone."

'Before I could even tell Beulah to show them into the
morning-room, an ebony cane came wagging dangerously
round the door unmindfully ready to put out an eye or strike
a breast, and a cracked unpleasant voice I had heard before
followed it:

' "No such thing! No such thing! Don't yer go to Chapel,
girl? Don't you fear yer Maker? I never asked to see yer
master. I told yer to tell him that his mother-in-law was
here. Here!" she repeated, striking the floor with her cane.
"Well?" she said, staring round at us. "Well? Ain't any of
yer got a word to say for yerselves? Don't any of you know
what to do when an old woman that's just lost her only child
comes into the room?"

' "Amelia!" said Mrs Livingstone in shamed protest.

' "I don't need you hitching round me with your ever-
lasting *Amelia, Amelia!*" she mimicked irritably.

' "Beulah, you may go," I said in a low aside. I glanced at
Lucy and she sprang forward.

' "Won't you please come and sit down?" she said
prettily, drawing out a chair. "You must be tired after your
journey."

' "How d'yer know where I've come from?" she countered. "D'yer think I had ter walk all the way?" she cackled.
But she heaved herself up on to the chair with a wriggle, and
stared round at us again like an evil child.

'I was in terror every moment that she would turn and address me in a way that would show we had met before. Yet although she stared round at us so, she did not appear to recognise us – perhaps she was immersed in the role she was playing, or perhaps the stroke of grief had made havoc of her memory.

'I said nervously to Mrs Livingstone:

' "Won't you have something to take? A glass of wine? Or some tea?"

'The old woman immediately struck her cane on the floor to command silence. The scene, it was at once evident, was to be played how she wished. We were to be intimidated.

'She said:

' "Which of you killed my daughter?"

'Said so unemphatically that the meaning of the words struck one like a piece of ice slithering down one's back, the same gasp of incredulous shock. The room moved round me, slowly, but with an effect of rushing. There was no untainted air to breathe. I clutched surreptitiously at the brocade curtains to support myself.

'I heard myself saying in a high-pitched unnatural voice:

' "Why, Mrs Falk, what are you talking about?"

'Hunched in her chair like a toad, she said, with a sharp glance at me:

' "One of you is responsible for my girl's death. One of you drove her to it. I know my girl, she wouldn't have killed herself for nothing; she had courage. But someone got at her. Someone made her think life was no longer worth living. Was it you?" she snapped, glittering at Oliver as though she had never seen him before.

'Oliver began to stammer wildly, as pale as a schoolboy caught by a master.

'Mrs Falk rapped Lucy's calves smartly with her cane.

' "Tell him to hold his tongue," she commanded. "Come! Do as I say."

' "Amelia, *don't!*" prayed Mrs Livingstone. "You're frightening the poor child!"

' "I'll thank you to keep yer mouth shut, Fanny; this is my affair! Come here, my pretty," she said, pulling Lucy to her. "You ain't afraid of me, are yer?" She stroked the long fair hair lovingly, her hand rasping the glittering tresses. "Eh, Goldilocks?" she said fondly.

' "No, Mrs Falk," said Lucy, holding still with stoical endurance while the hand like a puddock heavily caressed her hair.

' "Pretty enough in a silver-gilt way for a doll-faced niminy miss like yourself," she conceded, holding a bunch of it to the light, "but didjer ever see my Sophie's hair let loose?" she said in a hoarse whisper. "Like amber it was," she gloated. "Red amber! Wasn't it, Oliver? How it used to *shine* against her white skin! Didn't it, Oliver? Well, I daresay Mr Sheridan's thinking of it this minute, even if you've forgotten. Faithless fellow!" she chided. "Oh, it drew 'em, it drew 'em, like amber draws tissue," she chuckled. "Didn't it, Oliver? She knew the power of it. Didn't she, Oliver? I can see her now – younger than you by a long way," she said, gripping Lucy by the wrist, "shaking out her hair in the sunlight with such a knowing little look over her shoulder, and sure enough someone's heart would be caught in it like a fish is caught in a net. Oh, the little rascal! She learnt it all as greedily as she sucked my milk. *Never* give, I said to her, never give! Keep your thoughts, keep your heart, to yourself. Tell nothing! Trust nobody, not even yer old Ma, I said. Be proud, I said. Be hard. Make 'em pay for what they want; make 'em pay, every one of 'em, without mercy. The higher the price, the greater the value. People think it's the other way round, the fools; that price follows value: it don't. *I* taught her that. *I* taught her how to use her power. Oh, I taught her, I taught her to get her dues from life. It won't be for long that life will give you what you're after, don't waste yer time, my lass, I said; yer chance is only while yer young and pretty and can turn men's heads, once you become an ugly old wretch like yer Ma yer done for – remember that! Yes, I told her the truth about life. She could never reproach me for not telling her how to make the most of herself. *And* I showed her how she could enjoy herself at the same time; didn't I, Oliver, my pet? Ah, she was well satisfied, my Sophie!"

' "Was that why she took her own life?" I interrupted harshly, sickened by this half-insane monologue of debauchery.

'The head quivered and appeared to withdraw into the shoulders, the feathers trembling on its monstrous hat. But almost immediately the brown old face turned towards me and thrust out its square jaw:

' "Took her own life, did she? And what do you know about it, pray, miss? Were yer there? Were yer spying on her again like the – "

' "Oliver," I said clearly across this, "please fetch Papa!"

' "Oliver, don't budge!" she countermanded, with a wicked grin twisting her long, loose, purple lips. "Yer might hear something to yer advantage."

' "What have you come here for, Mrs Falk?" I said coldly. "I don't believe you've come to mourn your daughter at all; I believe you've only come to make trouble."

'She hitched herself forward in her chair like an angry dwarf. Her eyes blinked out fire like the dusty jewels on her bosom and fingers. Her head shook with the force of feeling contained in it, and the plumes on her hat nodded. She stretched out her raddled neck and exclaimed hoarsely, spittle foaming at the corners of her toad-lipped mouth:

' "I've come for revenge!"

'The curious thing was that nobody laughed at this absurd remark. I don't think anyone thought it in the least funny even. It was somehow horribly impressive. You see, we all believed her. Even Oliver did, I could see.

'I made a great effort and said:

' "Revenge won't help your daughter, Mrs Falk."

'She moved her head round slowly to where I stood against the light dauntlessly facing her. Her eyes were filmed. She looked ancient beyond humanity, with the ancientness of a stone, without heart, without feeling, that has but to endure the heat and rain and snow that falls on it impartially.

'She said dully:

' "My daughter is dead. She is not concerned with any of you now. I am the one who calls for revenge. It will give me something to live for."

' "Oh, hush, Amelia!" said Mrs Livingstone pitifully again. "You should have more respect for these good people in their sorrow. You shouldn't speak so to them, dear."

' "Then take me away, Fanny; I'm tired," she said on a sigh. "I'll come back another day."

'She clambered out of her chair and stumped away on her cane, ignoring us all equally.

'She descended the steps; hunched, hideous, and dreadfully pathetic.'

CHAPTER NINE

RENDEZVOUS

The afternoon sun pressed its red light against the figured apertures wrought in the brass lattice. It had been hot before; now it passed description. Mr Jones wondered how the indomitable old lady could talk so unflaggingly on and on in this blazing air. She sat there as placidly as a Buddha on a lotus, her knees spread a little apart and her hands on her thighs, a distant look dreaming on her fine, broad, old face. Perhaps she was so wrapt in the past that she was only conscious of the keen salted winds of Essex blowing about her. Himself wilted pitiably in the heat, he felt as though the marrow was melting in his bones. He tried to think of cool green things, of limpid becks and waterfalls spraying out rainbows as they tumbled.

But wherever her thoughts were, she was too good a hostess to neglect her guest's comfort. Or, at least, not for long.

'My poor friend, you look like an expiring fish panting on a slab,' she said, without malice, smiling across at him. 'Are you hot?'

'A trifle warm,' he admitted.

She struck a bell. And presently a servant shuffled in with a beaker of pressed limes foaming in sherbet. It was tart and delicious and blessedly grateful to the tongue. He would have liked to pour it over his burning head, but at that moment another domestic entered with a brazen vessel full of steaming towels which, kneeling down, he proceeded to wring out and fling scalding on Mr Jones's flesh. Just for a minute he was going to scream and then he was suddenly aware that it was remarkably pleasant.

'But I must, I really must, try a Turkish Bath when I get home,' he said to himself as he closed his eyes.

When he was refreshed she continued as though there had been no interruption.

'It was a few days after Mrs Falk's visit that I was obliged to go up to London to see my dentist. Harry went with me as escort. When we reached Liverpool Street Station we had nearly twenty minutes to wait.

'We sat in the waiting-room hardly speaking. Once Harry took my ungloved hand in his and said, "Why, Blanche, you're frozen!" I smiled at him faintly. "Funk," I murmured.

' "Let me stay with you, Blanche."

'I shook my head.

' "You must let me do this my own way, Harry dear. Please. I shall be all right. Come back for me in an hour. There's a good boy."

' "Papa wouldn't like it, if he knew, he said obstinately.

' "Gracious, if Papa knew!" I said with a little laugh that had a tremor of fear in it.

'Harry went away. And I walked slowly to the great white dial of the station clock, and as I went I fastened more securely the white rose I was wearing on my mantle.

'He was there waiting.

'I knew him at once – and I had been afraid I should not recognise him! I did not call him for a moment. I had just a minute before he should turn and see me in which to watch him while he was quite unconscious of being observed, in which to judge him.

'Then he caught sight of me and an astonished smile spread over his face and he held out his hands gladly.

' "Blanche Rose!" he cried.

' "Robert!" I said, smiling.

' "I just can't believe it! My little sister quite grown-up!"

' "Did you think you were going to meet a little girl?" I laughed.

' "Gee, I don't know what I thought," he laughed. "Oh, this is simply great!" he said, squeezing my arm. "Listen, we've got the deuce of a lot to talk over. Where can we go?"

' "Could we go to the buffet? We might have a cup of tea."

' "Oh, tea!" he said, and laughed again. "This terrible tea all the time, it's driving me crazy! But come on, sis, we'll manage one more cup for auld lang syne."

' "Now!" he said, when he had given the order. "I want to know all about everything."

'I rolled up my gloves carefully, not looking at him.

' "What do you want to know?" I said.

' "Well, to begin with, how the dickens did you find out it was me?" he said, and his eyes were watchful and not smiling any more.

' "I suppose I guessed," I said.

'Suddenly he noticed my fingers playing with my balled gloves and he exclaimed: "Why, sis, you're married!"

' "Good gracious, Robert, I should hope so. I'm going to have a baby!"

' "You are! By all that's wonderful!" he marvelled. He looked at my face, and said: "Happy, kid?"

' "Why, what an extraordinary question, Bob! Why ever shouldn't I be?"

'The waitress brought the tea and I was able to busy myself with pouring it out.

' "Tell me about yourself, Robert," I said.

' "Me? The old rolling stone! Nothing worth telling. Been in Canada most of the time."

' "So I gathered. Not married yet?"

' "Do I look that mossy?" he grinned. "Rolling stones don't marry, you know. Too busy negotiating the bumps."

' "Have you made a success of life, would you say? Are you happy?"

' "I'm still alive, ain't I?" he said comically. "But let's talk seriously, sis. The old man still hasn't forgiven me, eh?"

' "No," I said uncomfortably.

' "Shall you tell him you've seen me?"

' "Heavens, no!"

' "Won't have my name mentioned, is that it?" he said wryly.

'I bowed my head. I crumbled my bath bun on the plate. I said nervously:

' "Robert, what made you come back?"

'He gave a sour laugh.

' "I thought I'd see if I could screw out of the old man the shilling he cut me off with."

' "Do you need money?" I asked.

'He looked at me thoughtfully with Lucy's light blue eyes that I now saw were colder than hers and less transparent.

' "We'll talk of that another time. You haven't told me a word about Mama yet. How is she? Does she know you're here?"

'I stared.

' "Don't you know?" I said softly. "She's dead. She's been dead nearly six years." He went pale and I hesitated. Then I added in a whisper: "Papa married again." But when I raised my eyes I saw that he wasn't listening.

'He said quite casually:

' "Don't turn round, Blanche; someone is watching us. An oldish guy at a table about four rows back to the left."

'As he spoke, I took out a little pocket mirror from my vanity-bag and feigned to tidy my hair under the brim of my bonnet, moving the little mirror this way and that looking for the person Robert described. When I saw him I uttered an exclamation and half-rose from my seat.

' "Don't move!" said Robert between his teeth. "Who is it?"

'I looked at him in fear. But before I could speak to warn him, Mr Pierce was standing at our table. He put a hand on Robert's arm.

' "Mr Sheridan, alias Dunstable," he said, "I arrest you in connection with the death of Mrs Sheridan, and I am bound to warn you that anything you say may be used in evidence."

'For one moment Robert's eyes widened as though he

was going to do something incredibly violent, and then he gave me a terrible look, a smile I shall never forget:

' "*You* fixed this up!" he said. "And I walked into it neatly, didn't I? You see, I thought it would be quite safe to trust my own sister."

' "Robert, I didn't," I said faintly. "I swear I knew nothing about it." I wrung my hands.

'Mr Pierce said, "I hope you'll come quietly, sir, and not upset the lady by making a scene."

'People were already beginning to stare inquisitively at our table. I hid my burning cheeks in my hands.

' "Mr Pierce," I said in a shaking voice as he passed me with Robert, "how did you know? Even if you just followed me, how could you possibly know whom I was meeting?"

' "I saw this," said the policeman, laying before me on the table a tiny snipped-out newspaper cutting that I did not have to read. I knew what it said.

' "ROBERT, please meet me Liverpool St Station, Thursday, 11.30 a.m. under the clock. Shall be wearing white rose for you. BLANCHE."

'So I had been to blame after all. Now I had lost Robert altogether. I did not know where they had taken him. And I knew I could never expect him to respond to an appeal of mine again. Tears were still dripping through my fingers when Harry came back and found me, and took me home again.

'However, I did see Robert once more. It was at the resumed inquest. My heart nearly stopped when they said, "Call Robert Sheridan!" and he came in looking sullen and bitter.

'He was sworn in and the Coroner began by asking him if he was the son of Edward Sheridan.

' "Yes."

' "You have not lived at home for some years?"

' "That is correct."

' "Exactly how long is it that you've been away?"

' "Eight years."

' "What made you leave home?"

' "I quarrelled with my father."

' "Did he – turn you out?"

' "No, I ran away."

' "Did you hold any communication with your family during that time?"

' "No."

' "Could they have got into communication with you if they had so wished?"

' "No. They did not know where I was."

' "I see. Then am I right in suggesting that you had no means of knowing that your mother was dead or that your father had married again?"

' "Yes."

' "To turn to recent events. You decided to return to England, and shortly after your arrival you went down to Essex to visit your home. Will you tell the jury in your own words what then occurred?"

' "I asked to see my father," said Robert with a weariness as of a tale too often repeated, "but when he knew who it was, he refused to see me. So I asked to see Mrs Sheridan, meaning my mother. The maid said she was in the garden, and I went to look for her, thinking to surprise her. Instead I found this woman – I hadn't the ghost of an idea who she was – half-lying on the seat, and it didn't require any medical knowledge to see that she was dead."

' "Can we establish the time of this discovery?"

' "It was a quarter after four when I rang the bell of the house, so it could hardly have been much more than half after, I should imagine."

' "Pray continue. What happened then?"

' "I vamoosed p.d.q."

' "I beg your pardon?" said the Coroner.

' "I mean I did a bunk."

' "Why did you not get help or at least tell the house-hold?"

' "I was scared."

' "So you ran away?"

' "Yes."

' "Did you touch her or move the body at all?"

' "What should I want to touch her for? I could see she was dead."

' "Is it a fact that you are wanted by the police in Canada?"

' "Yes."

' "And it was in fact less from fear of being connected with Mrs Sheridan's death in some way than of being recognised by the police of this country, that made you flee?"

' "Yes," said Robert. And it was only when he turned to go that I realised why he kept his hands behind him all the time – it was because they were braceleted together. My heart burned with shame and grief within me. I thought, would these shameful disclosures never end? I was thankful Papa was not here; he had been excused from attending by a medical certificate.

'The Coroner had established that Sophia was already dead by half past four. The cyanide of potassium from Harry's poison-cupboard in the dark-room was brought out and there were deadening arguments I could not follow about quantities, measured in grains. Then various chemists were called and testified that none of the preparations bought from them by the deceased had contained prussic acid in any form.'

'One of them was shown a box of digestive powders and admitted they were put up by himself. They contained principally, he said, magnesia and soda bicarbonate. They were quite harmless. One powder tipped on the tongue and slowly dissolved in the mouth after meals; the dose to be repeated if relief was not obtained. Mr Pierce produced for the chemist the little square of paper that had fluttered from Sophia's skirt and the chemist identified it as the paper he used for his powders.

'The Coroner said since, as the doctor had testified, the deceased could not possibly have taken the powder *after* the cyanide of potassium, she must have taken it before. The jury had then to decide how the cyanide was administered – in what vessel or container – and whether it could have been self-administered, in these circumstances. They must take into consideration the state of mind of the deceased at the time, and also bear in thought that although the police had searched the surroundings very thoroughly, it was a possibility that the capsule, or whatever the cyanide had been contained in, might have fallen and rolled into some cranny where it had not yet come to light. Would they be justified in ruling out the possibility of suicide? And so on.

'Eventually the foreman of the jury stood up and said:

' "In accordance with the evidence we find the deceased died of cyanide poisoning, there is not sufficient evidence to determine how it was administered, but we think it must have been administered of deliberate intent by some person or persons as yet unknown."

'A verdict of Wilful Murder! I had not expected that, and I hardly knew how to get out of the courtroom on Oliver's arm. I had a terrified feeling we were going to be harried and persecuted by old Mrs Falk.

'I wanted to creep into the earth and hide. I could not imagine what was going to happen to us all now. There had been a MURDER in the family! We would be haunted by the malignant dead for the rest of our lives, it seemed.

'To begin with, the shock smoothed out all our jagged irritability. It had the strange effect of drawing us closer to one another in spirit, of uniting us against the world in a deep sympathy born of outrageous and unmentionable fear – it made us kind to one another as people were kind during the war. One went to sleep at night and woke up the next morning to a sense of perpetual accusation by unseen eyes. One wondered how long this lacuna of waiting could last, one wondered how much more of it one could possibly endure; yet all the while one dreaded that it would come to an end, with all one's apprehension of ultimate horror. Anything rather than that, one prayed; better this torment for the rest of one's life. The horror of the future hung over the present and made it intolerable, while its ultimate hidden shape advanced inexorably, minute by minute, like a monster in a nightmare,' said Miss Hine.

CHAPTER TEN

A WREATH OF CARNATIONS

'What was utterly horrible to me,' went on Miss Hine after a moment, 'was that I had lost all contact with Father. He did not come within our charmed circle of kindness. He avoided us all with a kind of horror. I think he was afraid. What he must have been pondering night and day was the unpleasing problem of Sophia's blatant infidelity. He tortured himself with wanting, and dreading, to know who her lover had been. And certainly the obvious answer was one of the two men she had mostly been with during his absence: in a word, either Harry or Oliver.

'You can picture the painfulness of the situation for him. To be betrayed by his own son had an ominously Biblical threat to it. It would be a catastrophe without solution. But would it be any better to find the adulterer one's own son-in-law, the husband of one's favourite child? He was afraid, I suppose, that I should read his fear in his eyes, and recognise the origin of it. So he avoided us all. Except Lucy. Little blonde adorable Lucy was safe. She was still a child, still confident, still natural, still wholly innocent and untouched by the destroying passion. I think her simple chatter soothed and diverted his mind.

'She and Edgar of course did not go to the funeral. The rest of us attended the bleak little ceremony. It was to be as quiet and as hurried as possible. It would have been a farce to make a spectacle of our mourning for the public. Clap up the whole business and have done with it as hastily as was compatible with dignity, I think we all felt. There were to be no mourners, no flowers, and by special arrangement with the vicar the funeral was to take place before early Communion, at seven o'clock in the morning, so that no one else could be present.

'At the best of times funerals are desolate experiences. But at that hour, in those circumstances, on a chilly morning in late September, when fingers and noses were nipped by the first frosts, that were resolved into diamond fragments beading the webs slung between the broad-leaved green spires by the lychgate, there was something harsh about the scene, like a crude woodcut or Courbet's painful *Funeral at Ornans*. A mist was coming in off the sea and we stood huddled in our black by the wet yellow clay, looking pinched and dejected.

'I thought how pathetically new and bare the sand-coloured coffin looked as it swayed towards us on the pall-bearers' shoulders, and how I should hate to be shut away in something so unfriendly. I have said there were to be no flowers, but as they lowered the coffin, a large wreath of scarlet carnations slipped tipsily to the ground. I stole a frightened glance at Oliver. For who else would have dared to do such a thing against Papa's express orders? And I realised at once that by the mere doing of it he was declaring as clearly as words that the dead woman had been to him something more than the cousin-relationship they had pretended. I dared not look at Papa. But when Oliver at last turned his eyes towards mine I saw that his bewilderment matched my own.

'The vicar blew his nose, adjusted his pince-nez, and began reading the service by the graveside in a hurried undertone, rather as if he was checking his laundry-list. Perhaps he was only afraid of catching cold, but it made the business more ignoble than it was already.

'It was as they swung the coffin down into the grave that a sound behind me made me turn, and I saw them – standing behind us a little way away, as though we had the prior claim! Mrs Livingstone and Mrs Falk.

'Mrs Livingstone had a handkerchief to her face, but Mrs Falk was glaring at us baldly above her twisted cynical mouth. Of course the wreath was hers; she could not know and would not care that to us the hypocrisy of flowers struck an unseemly note.

'They stood there in our path awaiting us as we came away. Mrs Falk's voice rose harsh and clamant on the still air:

' "A pity our first meeting should be such a sad occasion, Mr Sheridan."

'He had only just replaced his tall hat and now he bared his head again, which had so thickened with white in these last days. Plainly he had no idea who she was and was too engrossed in his thoughts even to wonder; he would have passed her by, but she halted him with a hand on his sleeve.

' "You don't know who I am!" she said with a queer sort of triumph.

'He said:

' "Madam, you cannot know, but you are intruding upon a private interment."

'I darted forward:

' "Papa, this is Mrs Falk. Sophia's mother," I said urgently.

' "Your mother-in-law, my dear, dear boy," she said with the ludicrous effect of a crocodile weeping over its prey.

'A look of disgust passed across Papa's stern impassive features and did not escape her sharp old eyes.

' "*I* taught Sophia to be ashamed of me," she said with that familiar arrogant thrust of her brown protruding jaw, "that's why you never met me before. It would have frightened you away, eh?" she leered. She chumbled for a while, creaking into another phase like a car shifting gears. "But now, my dear boy, our loss has brought us together. You are all I have left in the world," she said, the old lips puckering and folding.

' "What is it you want from me, madam?" Papa asked with grim patience.

' "For Sophia's sake," she mumbled. "She would have wanted you to – "

'Papa looked at her with hatred.

' "I owe Sophia nothing," he said harshly. "I have paid my debt to her fully and finally. Let me pass, madam!"

' "An old woman . . . " she whimpered after him.

'We scuttled after him, eager to escape. But at the lych-gate I glanced behind me and saw her leaning once again on Mrs Livingstone's arm, staring after us with so malign an expression that my flesh goose-skinned all over.'

'What did she want?' asked Mr Jones, puzzled.

'Did I not make it clear? She wanted money. Sophia had been keeping her all the time on Papa's money. She was frightened about what was to become of her now, naturally enough. But the money had been eased from Papa's pockets on other pretexts; it is no difficult matter for an adored young wife to get money from her husband for pretty clothes, but not many husbands are so eager to support a mother-in-law. Sophia was clever, she managed to get the pretty clothes too,' Miss Hine explained.

'I should have thought Mr Bridgewater would have been a much simpler problem for the old lady to tackle?'

'Oliver? I quite agree. Unfortunately, however, Oliver hadn't any money. It would have been useless to blackmail him. She tried that later,' said Miss Hine drily.

'It was surely a little crude of her to try and rush your father into it there and then, before she had even met him properly and while they were at the very grave-side?' he suggested.

'She was not a clever person though she was endowed with abundant cunning. And remember, this was the second time she had tried to approach him, she was beginning to lose her nerve a little; she made a wild grab and missed!' The old lady slipped a striped cushion behind her head and closed her eyes.

Mr Jones waited politely. At last he said tentatively that he hoped he hadn't tired her.

'Not at all,' she said without opening her eyes. 'I'm thinking.'

'Thinking?'

'About what happened next,' she explained.

The cricket in its little paper cage resumed its singing, as if to fill the silence.

Presently Miss Hine opened her clear blue eyes and said: 'Harry went up to business as usual after breakfast that day. It would hardly have been decent for Papa to go. Instead he took Lucy with him and went for a long tramp across the flats and salt marshes. She came back with the guilty smile and richly glowing averted eyes of the mischief-maker. I wondered what she had been saying to Papa. She ran up to the nursery. Papa followed her more slowly. But when I went up later, Lucy was alone, curled in the big cane chair in front of the nursery fire with Strickland's *Queen Elizabeth* open in her hand. As soon as she saw me she became deeply absorbed in it and did not hear me call her name. I put my hand on her shoulder.

' "Lucy! What are you up to?" I said.

'The shoulder shrugged under my hand.

' "You can see – reading."

' "You know very well what I mean, Lucy," I said. "You've been up to something with Papa."

'She bit her lip and flirted the pages of her book impatiently.

' "Oh, Blanche, do let me alone! I want to get on with this. I've got to do three chapters for Miss Hughes tomorrow."

' "What was Papa catechising you about?" I demanded.

' "Why don't you ask him, if you want to know?" she said pertly.'

'As soon as Harry returned from Town, Papa sent for him. I felt anxious and waited about quarter of an hour for him to come down and tell me about it. It was so long since Papa had wanted to speak to any of us except Lucy. After a while I went out to take a turn in the garden. It was while I was pacing to and fro, lost in my thoughts, that I was roused by a wild shriek from the house, and I looked up to see Harry's face contorted with fury as he shook Lucy by the shoulders so that her head wobbled helplessly. It was from her that the shrieks came as she pressed back against the sill.

‘ "Let me *go!* Let me *go!*" she yelled; while Harry shouted: "You little devil! You wicked little devil!"

‘I tried to call, "Harry, *don't!*" But I was too late. I don't know what happened. I could not see. I only saw Lucy's long tresses spread out upon the air and her body slowly turning, first like some great trussed bird and then the arms and legs unfolding in the pale evening light like the incredible limbs of some groping prehistoric insect. There came from her a thin deflated scream before she hit the ground.

‘She lay on the path, motionless.

‘ "Lucy!" I said, kneeling beside her, my face blurred with tears. I thought she was dead, until she began to groan. I dared not touch her. I looked up to where Harry still stood at the window, transfixed, white as a clock in the gathering twilight.

‘ "Harry!" I called softly. "Run quickly – "

‘ "Have I killed her?" he said in a dead voice.

‘ "She's still alive, but she's unconscious. You must get help at once."

‘And all at once we were back in the nightmare of a few weeks back, with Dr Scott and the policemen. By a little miracle no bones were broken except for her collar-bone. She was chiefly suffering from a very severe concussion. She was put to bed and a nurse installed. Papa sat by her bedside looking grey. I wanted to comfort his sad heart but did not know what to say. Something was irrecoverably broken between us. I could no longer be natural with him, I had become afraid.

‘Papa saw the police first. He was closeted with them for a considerable while. They sent for Harry next. He came out white to the lips. He had only time to say to me hopelessly as I passed: "They've got my poems! They think I killed her!"

'I entered the morning-room where the police were waiting, with my mind in a turmoil. I knew he had written poetry to Sophia, but I had no notion of its content or how far it committed him. And what worried me was what he meant by his last sentence: "They think I killed her!" Who was the *her*? Did they suspect him of killing Sophia or Lucy? It made a difference, because Sophia was dead, and that meant *murder*. Whereas Lucy, I suppose, could only have been "attempted homicide". I wished dearly I had had time to ask him a few questions, to prepare myself for the policemen's queries.

'Mr Pierce pulled out a chair for me almost jovially, as though we were old friends.

' "I understand," he said, "that you were an eye-witness to what occurred and we should like to have your account of it. It must have been a very unpleasant shock for you, Mrs Bridgewater; take your time."

' "I'm all right, thank you," I said. "But I'm afraid I don't really know what did happen. I was taking a little constitutional as I always do if it's fine about that time of day. And I heard a scream. I looked up and saw my sister at the window. She appeared to be backing away from my brother, as it might be in play. I think she did not realise how close she was to the open window. I wanted to call out and warn her, but before I could do so, she fell." I put my hands over my eyes.

' "In your opinion she fell rather than was pushed?"

' "I did not see my brother push her."

' "Did he touch her at all?"

' "I think he had a hand on her shoulder and she was wriggling to get free," I said consideringly.

' "Your brother says that he had her by both shoulders and was shaking her."

' "Oh! Did he?" I said indifferently.

' "That was not how it seemed to you?"

' "If he says it was like that it must have been."

' "Could you see your sister's expression?"

' "No. She had her back to the window."

' "Your brother then, was facing you? Am I right?"

' "Yes."

' "Did he look as if he was only playing?" Mr Pierce said deliberately.

' He certainly did not look as if he was going to push her out of the window," I countered tartly.

' "Do you know what they were quarrelling about?"

' "I've no idea. I did not even know they were quarrelling."

' "Thank you, ma'am; we won't keep you any longer."

'There was a policeman stationed outside Lucy's door, waiting to be called the instant she came to herself. And presently his colleagues went away and left him there on duty.

'I went all over the garden looking for Harry in the dark and calling him softly. I found him in the stable loft, sitting moodily on a bin of oats, drinking Dutch gin out of a bottle the stable-boy had procured for him. There was a lantern in the straw beside him.

' "I've been looking for you everywhere," I said. "Make room for me, Harry."

' "Leave me alone, Blanche! I don't want company."

'I knelt down clumsily in the straw at his feet.

' "Harry,' I said, touching him gently. "What happened?"

' "Ask the police," he answered surlily. "They know all about it."

'I said timidly, "Do they think you – you were trying to – kill her?"

'The quiet gloom was suddenly torn across by Harry's strident unkind laughter.

' "Why not? Might as well be hanged for a sheep as a lamb! I would have killed the little beast for two pins, I swear." He tipped up the bottle again from bravado and to avoid meeting my eye.

' "Why were you so angry with her, Harry? What had she done?"

' "Know what she'd done, little beast? Shown my poems, stolenem out of private place and shownem to Pa . . . Old man sent for me, asked me straight out, 'thout a word of warning, what the hell – pardon! – was all about. Kewsed me delibritly of being in love with her . . . Hated her, I said, cruellest woman alive! Good thing she's dead! No more damage to other people. Thass what I said . . . Meaning of these outrageous pomes, sir? he said. Hel' my tongue. Wise old bird, the owl . . . He said, that any son of mine . . . !" Harry struck an attitude and nearly fell off the bin. "Hey!" he cried. "Give me back my boddle!"

' "I want a drink, Harry, don't be stingy," I said, holding it in my lap so that the liquid trickled out of the neck into the pool of shadow at my skirts.

' "Go on," I whispered. "What about Lucy?"

' "All her fault, the beastly little sneak. Frightened the life out of her. Meant to half murder her but the silly little ass fell."

' "It was an accident. You didn't push her, Harry, did you?"

' "Stupid donkey pulled away. Only giving her a good shaking. Gimme back my boddle, Blanche!"

' "Don't drink any more, dear."

' "Better a merry ole drunkard be
      Than swing alive from the murderer's tree!"

he chortled. "Made that up 'bout the Sheridans. All rotten. Disown Robert, disown Harry. Blackguards," he muttered more and more incoherently, his huge shadow lurching across the cobwebbed whitewashed roof. I closed the door of the lantern and made my way down the ladder.

'I don't know what time Harry went to bed. I never heard him come in. But he was himself the next day, though unnaturally pale and subdued.

'Lucy did not regain consciousness till noon that day. It happened we were all there in her room, except Oliver, when she opened her eyes. The nurse bent over and spoke to her softly. She did not answer, her eyes looked vague and unfocused. Papa picked up her limp childish hand and patted it gently. His face loomed before her and suddenly she seemed to recognise it and smiled. The nurse persuaded her to take some broth. She watched us with a puzzled look as she absently imbibed it, wondering what we were all doing there. The policeman came to her side with his notebook. A look of fear flicked into the child's eyes.

' "Now, miss, can you tell us what happened?"

' "Happened?" she said in a wisp of a voice.

' "What is the last thing you remember?" he suggested.

'She thought painfully for a moment. And then, "Harry . . . " she whispered.

' "What about Harry?"

' "Very angry with me. Up in the nursery. I was frightened." She moved her head from side to side. "He hurt me," she whimpered.

' "What did you do?"

' "I said, *Don't, Harry! Don't!*" she said in a small terror-stricken voice.

' "Why were you so afraid? Can you remember?"

' "I was afraid . . . afraid . . . He was hurting . . . And then I saw the ground coming after me," she said, shrinking into the pillows with a look of terror. "I fell out of the window, didn't I?"

'The nurse said, "Now that is enough, if you please. We shall be getting hysterical in a minute."

' "One question more," said the constable. "How did you come to fall, miss, do you know?"

' "I don't understand," she said childishly.

' "I mean, missie, did you slip and lose your balance in some way? Or did it feel as if you were . . . pushed?"

'She looked across the room at us.

' "I was pushed," she said clearly. "Harry pushed me."

'Harry thrust forward and as he passed her bedside spat out scornfully: "Liar! Little liar!" and pushed from the room as the nurse said in brisk offended tones:

' "Now, now, that's quite enough of that! I can't have my patient upset." And she shooed the lot of us from the room.'

CHAPTER ELEVEN

MEMORY OF THE FIRST MRS SHERIDAN

'I suppose it was the silly child's idea of revenge; she could not have known what she was implying; she could not have intended to harm her brother,' the old lady said meditatively. 'We cannot now know whether they had enough evidence to have arrested poor Harry anyway. I mean, for the murder of his stepmother. For that must have been in the back of their minds all the time, of course, once they had seen the verses he had composed about her – or rather, what he felt about her. You know what policemen are like; the mere writing of poetry is suspect to them, regardless of content.

'Perhaps they imagined that if he was arrested he might break down and confess. They did have something to go on after all, one must admit in all fairness to them. He had plainly been in love with her, and the love was of an unhappy illicit nature (*vide* the poems); moreover he was the person who owned the cyanide, had even purchased some only a short while before the catastrophe, and knew of necessity its deadly qualities. Whatever his motive may have been, he was clearly the person who had most knowledge and opportunity to obtain the poison.

'Yes, I can see their point now, though I admit I could not then. Poor Harry, I was there when they arrested him, "for causing Lucy Sheridan bodily harm of malicious intent". He said nothing, but he went a deathly white and looked across at me.

'I said, "Harry dear, it's a mistake. Of course it's a mistake. We all know you didn't do it. Don't be afraid!"

' "I shall never come back," he answered.

'I was shocked.

' "Harry! Dear Harry! Of course you will," I said, clinging to him.

' "I shall not come back here again," he insisted. "Too much has happened. Tell Father – " he began and then he shrugged his shoulders. "No. What does it matter what he thinks?" he said wearily and let them lead him away.

'I went straight to Lucy at once.

' "They're taking Harry away," I said gravely.

'She held a lock of hair across her face and squinted at me through it.

' "Oh?" she said, measuring the tress down her nose.

' "You've succeeded nicely."

' "In what?" she asked with careful indifference.

' "In ruining your own life, as well as your brother's."

' "I don't know what you mean," she said sulkily.

'She was a little girl, you see, coming to the age where one's head is full of romance. I said, "Do you imagine any man is going to marry a girl whose brother has been in prison?"

'At that she pushed the hair off her face and sat up, round-eyed.

' "Prison!" She stared at me wildly. "Blanche!" she quavered.

' "Of course," I said. "Of course he must go to prison. You told the police that he pushed you out of the window when you were quarrelling."

'She burst into a torrent of grief.'

' "He didn't!" she cried. "He didn't! He didn't. Make them bring him back, Blanche! Tell them I didn't mean it. I made a mistake . . . I made a mistake!"

'The police were annoyed with Lucy, naturally enough, but there was nothing they could do. They had to let him go. They could not hold him on that charge, and they had not accumulated enough evidence, I suppose, to hold him on any other.

'So Harry came home – despite what he said. He could not do otherwise, poor angry boy, for until the crime was solved no one in the household was allowed to leave the neighbourhood. I don't believe he cared a bit about the police suspecting him, I think it gave him a certain sardonic amusement. And after all it was their job. What he did mind terribly, with all the proud innocence of youth, was that Father could bring himself to imagine for an instant that his own son would have betrayed him. Under their proper love for each other the long-smouldering antagonism caused by Sophia flamed up suddenly into hatred. He now hated his father as much as Papa hated him. All he wanted now was to leave home and Papa and all of us behind him for ever, he burned to get away.

'He stuck it sullenly, doggedly, for three days, and then in the dark interlude between moons, some time in the middle of the night, he disappeared. He left the house silently, without a sign. He left no word behind him, even for me. Apparently he took nothing with him except, I suppose, a few private papers. His clothes were all left hanging in the closet, like the abandoned shells of an old life, something he would no longer have any use for.

'Harry's disappearance threw us into the wildest confusion. We feared he had made away with himself. If he had even left the briefest note . . . And the police refused to believe that we were none of us privy to his departure. They were furious, with the ludicrous fury of a cat who has let a mouse slip through her paws and escape.

'For a week at least we lived in dread of hearing that his body had been washed up somewhere along the coast. Then there was a rumour that a carter had given him a lift five miles from Harwich. But nothing more came of that. (It was years before I heard what had happened: it seems he had walked to Harwich, arriving in the early hours just when the port was beginning to stir and had immediately signed on with a merchantman bound for Penang.)

'Meanwhile we could not know whether he had run away or was dead. And although I was stunned by the shock of it, I was also aware of a creeping shameful surge of relief. For I imagined that now the investigation would be closed.

Wouldn't the police regard Harry's flight or suicide as a declaration of guilt? Wouldn't they assume that from lack of evidence the case could not be pursued any further? Alas, the police are a breed of bulldogs; they never let go. I did not dream that they were still making their enquiries. I had even begun to hope the affair was quietly and unobtrusively blowing over, exhausting itself.

'But there were two things I had not realised.

'One was that nothing was ever going to be the same again. That life would never again be normal for any of us. That people never forget.

'I had taken the landau to the village, because I was beginning to look ungainly, and stopped at Cornstalks', the haberdashers, for some small necessities. It was buzzing with voices when I entered and made my way to the counter; I saw Mrs Gifford, Mrs Avery, Miss Nuthall turning their heads away as I came towards them; only the assistant was left at the counter I visited, all the ladies had melted away; I became suddenly conscious that the shop was heavily silent, as though it was full of wax dummies watching me from the backs of their heads. I found it required an enormous effort to complete my business, and when I got back to the carriage my legs were trembling.

'That unfortunate little expedition made me wonder for the first time what was going to happen to us all. I knew my husband was inwardly chafing to get away, though he scarcely spoke to me except to answer when I spoke. All day he would lie in sullen apathy on the striped sofa in the drawing-room, drinking brandy and seltzer and pretending to study one of his law-books, but his eyes would gaze vacantly at a page for an hour before he would remember to turn it.

'So I went to Papa and said I must speak to him. I forced him to listen. I told him that we should have to leave this house, this village, and start life again in some place where we were quite unknown just as soon as the investigation was concluded.

'He looked at me as if I were some impertinent stranger.

' "What for?"

' "Papa, you have not been out for a long while, not since . . . you do not know how people . . . this scandal has made them talk . . . "

' "They say? What say they? Let them say," quoth Papa indifferently.

' "It is hateful," I muttered. I bowed my head. "I did not want to tell you this, but three people cut me to-day: Mrs Gifford, Mrs Avery and Miss Nuthall."

' "Do you imagine that a pack of chattering females can frighten me out of my home, my dear girl?" he said in his heavy tired voice.

'I said unhappily:

' "Oliver wants to leave just as soon as we are allowed to. I expect he will want to live in London. I shall have to go with him."

' "Of course, of course."

' "I can't leave you here alone," I said desperately.

' "Why not, pray?" he asked with a shadow on his face like a smile.

' "I can't leave you shut up here alone to become a sort of hermit."

' "My dear child, what can it matter what becomes of me now? I am an old man with nothing left to look forward to but death. My life is over."

'I flew to him.

' "Papa, don't say that! You mustn't! You mustn't be so unhappy. We'll help each other to forget all the terrible things that have happened. Please say we will, Papa! I couldn't bear to live without you, indeed I couldn't!"

'He lifted my arms away.

' "Nonsense, my dear!" he said coldly. "You are young. All your life is still before you. You have your husband, and the future of your child to live for. It is your duty to put the past behind you and consider them."

'My heart's beating was an agonising pain in my breast. I stood before him stupidly like a stone and said faintly:

' "Papa, what have I done? Don't you love me any more?"

'He rested his eyes consideringly for a moment or two on my white face, as though the question had not occurred to him before. Then he said:

' "I am not able to love you. I am no longer able to care for anyone – or anything. When once one's heart is dead one has nothing left to love with."

'People talk so lightly about their hearts being broken, yet they still love other people. But when one's heart is really broken it can contain no more love for anyone. Yet I could not believe Papa, I could not believe he had ceased to love me for ever. I thought he must be angry with me, I thought I must have offended him in some way. I went weeping to my room and flung myself down on the bed. I wept because he was angry and I did not know why, and because his breast had been like a defensive wall when I had tried to embrace him and he had unlatched my arms. I refused to admit that there was to be no place for him in the future, that would have been too desolating; he'll change his mind, I thought. I'll make him change his mind.

'That was how I came to realise the first of the two things; that life was never going to be the same for us again. The second tremendous thing, I had not before realised, was that my own precious father was the natural and inevitable suspect of having murdered Sophia.

'When all the fuss of enquiry did not die down after Harry's disappearance, I learned that police interest was centring on Papa. For all I know, their attentions to Harry may merely have been a cover for their real investigation. Of course if Papa had known Sophia was going to have some other man's child, even I could see there would be grounds for suspecting him; but because we had all in our different ways and for our different reasons tried so hard to keep it from him, the notion had really never entered my head before.

'Almost overnight the village was a-buzz with rumours.

It seemed to have been flooded with anonymous letters. Naturally one was not sent to us. But we saw it nevertheless. One kind lady "came as a friend", as she put it, to show it me, she "thought I ought to see it".

'She put back her veil and said she frankly had no idea whether she ought to take it to the police or not. It seemed to her they ought to know, but . . . Such a disgusting calumny! What did I think?

'It was written on sheets from a child's penny exercise-book, printed in large trembling capitals that asked outrageously:

' "HOW DID THE FIRST MRS SHERIDAN DIE? PRAPS THE DOCTOR DIDNT OUGHT TO HAVE SIGNED THE CERTISSICATE SO HASTY? WHAT ARE THE POLICE GOING TO DO ABOUT IT? WHY DONT SOMEONE LOOK INTO IT? MURDRERS DIDNT OUGHT TO BE LET GO SO EASY."

'My fingers were shaking so atrociously I could scarcely tear up this wicked sheet. I tore it across and across, till it was too small ever to have been put together again.

' "That's what I think," I said, with a white smile.

' "My dear," said the lady, deeply shocked. "Ought you to have done that? I mean, wasn't it evidence?"

' "Evidence of what?" I asked coldly.

' "I think one of the gentlemen should have seen it first," she remonstrated.

' "Then why didn't you ask to see one of them instead of me? You should have shown it to Mr Sheridan," I said bitterly.

'She fanned herself rapidly with her card case.

' "Dear me! Dear me! Of course I am not for a moment suggesting that there is a word of truth in the horrid thing. But – this is all so terrible for you, my dear Mrs Bridgewater, you are so young – I do think the best thing is to be absolutely frank about meeting these accusations, if one has nothing to be afraid of. Otherwise you'll find, I'm afraid, they leave nasty little festering places. It is natural to be impulsive when one is young. But take the advice of an older woman: it does not do." She pulled her veil over her smile and rose.

'I thanked her politely.

'She said pensively:

' "Perhaps if I had done my duty I would have taken it to the police. But it seemed only fair to let you know what you were up against. Good-bye, Mrs Bridgewater." She nodded coolly and was gone.

'She need not have worried. Someone else did their duty and took their copy of the anonymous letter to the police to make sure they saw it. I wonder what the police thought of it? I wonder if they would have done anything about it if it had been left to them and nothing else had happened?

'For – it was too horrible! – it seemed that the village was clamouring for an exhumation. It was being said that Papa had "got rid" of Mama. You cannot imagine, Mr Jones, how ridiculous and terrifying that sounded. They were saying that Papa had *poisoned her* . . . too. You have no idea the terror and disgust one feels when little by little everything that has ever happened to one is raked up again to have some pejorative meaning placed on it. In the lives of the most respectable among us are hidden things we could not bear another person to know. Not because they are wicked, but because they are sacred. Mama's was sacred in that way to both Papa and myself.

'Yet the most innocent acts and motives somehow look false beneath the theatrical limelight of village gossip. Twist and turn as one may, one cannot evade it . . . Any more than I could evade the recollection of Mama's small panting face, exhausted with vomiting, sallow against her pillows,' recalled the old woman soberly.

'At last,' she continued, 'I ventured to go and see Mr Gifford – the husband of the lady who had cut me recently

in the haberdashers; they had both been great friends of
Mama's, and it was for her sake, in her name, that I went to
ask him if he could do nothing to stop this wretched scan-
dalising.

' "My dear young lady," he said, "what can *I* do?"

' "Why, you could tell them how wicked, how monstrous,
it is to suggest such a thing. You knew Mama. You know
how much Papa loved her. Can you imagine him poisoning
her? Or even wanting to? Why, he was heart-broken when
she died. Absolutely heart-broken," I insisted. "For four
years he cut himself off from life entirely in his grief. Why
should he have done that if it was not sincere? . . . And then
these wicked people say . . . how can they *think* such
things?"

' "A man has always got enemies, even though he may
not be aware of them," Mr Gifford said quietly.

' "Enemies?" I echoed in surprise. And at once I had a
picture of old Mrs Falk in the churchyard. This was her
malevolence. How was it I had not seen it before? She would
see to it that somebody suffered, guilt or no guilt. And the
person she would like best to injure, accuse, and punish,
would be none other than her dead daughter's husband.
How stupid of me not to have seen it before! I leaned forward eagerly:

' "If I tell you who has spread this slander . . . " I began.
'He held up his hand.

' "Please!" he said. "Nothing is to be gained by accusations – they will help no one."

' "You could force them to stop. You could threaten them
with prosecution. That would frighten them. They would
listen to you, you're a Justice of the Peace," I urged.'

' "Alas," he said and shook his silvery head, "I fear it has
gone too far for that."

'I said:

' "Mr Gifford, tell me the truth! Do you believe Papa
could have poisoned Mama?"

'He seemed to consider for an age, and then at last said,
"No."

' "Then there must be some way of stopping this indecent talk, and you must help me find it," I declared.

' "There is only one way to do that," said Mr Gifford. "If you do really want it stopped."

' "I do! I do!" I cried.

' "It is for your father's innocence to be proved. Then there will be nothing more to say."

' "But how?"

' "Your father must demand an exhumation himself to clear his name."

'I stared. I shrank back into the wing of the armchair.

' "I couldn't tell Papa that," I stammered. "To desecrate Mama's grave! He never would."

' "What has he to fear?" said Mr Gifford in a level tone.

' "N-nothing, of course. It isn't that. But, don't you see, if it was only to clear his name, he would never permit such a thing. He doesn't care any longer, he doesn't care about anything. All this," I said with a gesture, "has completely broken him up." I could not prevent my own voice breaking as I realised the truth of my words. "If you could see him now, you would weep, he has become so old and weary and dead-looking."

'But Mr Gifford did not weep. He only answered:

' "He may have to permit it, young lady."

' "What do you mean, sir?"

' "He will be given no choice in the matter if an exhumation order is asked for and the Home Secretary grants it. Myself, I think it is the best thing that could happen, if you want my opinion." He studied his fingernails and added: "You can tell your father I said so."

' "You mean, it is going to happen, Mr Gifford?" I said quietly, resting my anxious eyes on his.

' "You must not ask me questions I have no right to answer," he said.

'So then I knew.

'And I was afraid. That was the root of the matter. I had become infected with their horrible evil thoughts, and I was in a panic at the idea of an exhumation because I dreaded what they might discover. Not that for half a split-second would I have allowed myself to fancy Papa had really tried to poison Mama. But who knows what could happen inside a person's body after years underground? I imagined innocent substances commingling to become some deadly poison, and that sort of thing. And if once poison was established in poor Mama's cadaver I knew nothing could save Papa.

'And behind that fear lay the deeper fear of what Papa might do when he learned of the impending exhumation. I thought he might . . . I don't know what I thought, but I was distracted for him. I determined that he should not hear of it from me; I would not be a messenger of bad tidings.

'But in fact when he did learn of it he did nothing at all. He was like a trapped lion, roped and badgered, who cannot believe the indignity of his fate.

'The worst of it was that even if the exhumation should prove a blank, Father would still not be exempt from the suspicion of having murdered his second wife. I wondered how that suspicion was ever to be cleared away? Certainly, he could not live out the rest of his days with the mystery of Sophia's death hanging round his neck like an accursed albatross . . . the eternal, inescapable accusation! More impossible yet for me to contemplate was the idea of Father, my Beloved Hero, facing the accusation and standing trial. Rather than that, I almost think I would have given myself up in his stead. Indeed, that was the only possible solution, the real culprit must be found!'

CHAPTER TWELVE

A SUM OF OLD PAPERS

'Have you ever been present at an exhumation?' the old woman asked Mr Jones in the tone of one who asks, 'Have you ever had tea at the Palace, I wonder?' 'No, I suppose not,' she answered herself, 'but you can imagine for yourself the sombre setting with the great black yew trees blotting out the sky and the cold mournful sound of the grave-diggers' spades striking into the stony clay. And then in one corner of the churchyard, like some enormous ghostly Chinese lantern resting on the ground, an arrangement of canvas screens across which huge shadows blunder perpetually, as though a moth were blundering about the candle inside the Chinese lantern. And one tries not to picture the gruesome little scene within, as brilliant to the imagination as some dark glinting old painting of body-snatchers or anatomists. One tries vainly not to think about that pretty soft hair, so life-like and familiar on the bleached temples. One tries not to imagine scalpels propped within the hollow pelvis. One tries not to wonder what these unknown men with their secret intent faces will find in those shrivelled organs.'

'Really!' protested Mr Jones. 'Must you be so macabre?'

'How else is one to deal with a macabre subject?' she countered. 'However, if it alarms you we need not pursue it,' she said agreeably, like a kindly old nanny, and simply would not listen when he tried to explain that it was not alarm but something more subtle and fastidious.

But while he was resisting her cool imputation they were interrupted by a neat gentleman in white drill, who salaamed, was given permission to speak, and spoke. The old lady listened, nodded once or twice, and dismissed him.

But something about the airiness with which she did it struck a sudden doubt in Mr Jones's mind.

'What was that?' he asked sharply as the man disappeared.

Nanny looked mild disapproval at this breach of good manners.

'I wondered,' said Mr Jones sheepishly, 'if it was anything to do with my plane. I really am getting a little anxious,' said he, though the truth was that this was the first time it had entered his thoughts for some hours. 'I wonder if I should stroll across and see how he's getting on? Might stir him up a bit; they do slack, these beggars, don't they?'

'It's all right,' said Miss Hine. 'It will be quite ready when you are.'

He gave the bland old soul a searching look.

'That fellow came to tell you the plane was ready now, didn't he?'

'As a matter of fact, he did.'

'Then I must go!' he said, springing up.

'What's the hurry?' enquired the old lady calmly.

'We must get off before dark. I don't think Ras Ali is a very good pilot.'

'But it's not six yet. There's two hours to sunset. Plenty of time. Besides, you can't expect the man to fly off through the night without anything in his stomach and not even an hour's rest. Be reasonable, my dear sir.'

'Of course, of course. I suppose not,' said Mr Jones, uneasily. 'But I'm afraid Mahmoud Kahn will be worrying about what has happened to us. Even if we're not hopelessly off route, as I fear, we're already hours late.'

'Not he!' said Miss Hine robustly. 'It would take more than a trifle like a missing plane to trouble Mahmoud Kahn, believe me. Why, all the caves of the ocean and desert places of the earth are littered with the bones of the wretched tutors and secretaries who have been engaged by Mahmoud Kahn and never arrived to take up their duties. I assure you, he makes nothing of it. If a tutor doesn't arrive,

Mahmoud Kahn simply engages another by post.'

'I have to be back in London by October the 17th,' said Mr Jones with a pale look.

'I shall be so interested to know if you arrive,' said Miss Hine with something like a gush. 'You must give me your address! Now, promise!'

Mr Jones stared incredulously at this phlegmatic ghoul.

'You don't really think,' he began, and stopped.

'Don't worry, I shall have a very powerful spell made to protect you. You will be quite safe. I have an excellent wizard,' she assured him, in exactly the same tone she had used to describe her chauffeur and her cook. 'Now, do sit down again and be comfortable.'

'Do you mean you actually do believe in wizards and spells and things?' asked the young man cautiously.

She smiled placidly.

'Well, well, well,' she said. 'There's no telling what you can make people believe. But I think we shouldn't waste any more time, if you want to hear the rest of my story.'

'I do indeed,' said Mr Jones, for there was no denying the old woman was as crazy as your best girl's spring hat.

Miss Hine clasped her hands lightly in her lap and immediately resumed:

'I saw that the important thing was for me to stop, by some means or other, that old fiend Mrs Falk's mouth. I knew she was still with her sister, Mrs Livingstone, in the house at the shady edge of the village.

' "Ah," she said with rich satisfaction when she saw me, "I thought you'd come. Said so, didn't I, Fanny? Be off and ask that gal of yours to make her some tea. The special tea, Fanny!" she bawled after her. "Now then, whatyer want?"

' "This is not a social visit, Mrs Falk," I began sternly.

' "Never supposed it was," she retorted irrepressibly. "Yer've come because yer want something. I know your kind," she said with grand contempt.

' "I want you to stop blackguarding my father's name for a crime he never committed," I said coldly.

' "Me? What's it to do with me?" she said, opening her eyes so that I could see their yellow whites.

' "It is useless for you to pretend you are not at the bottom of it all. I assure you I would not have come, Mrs Falk, if I had not had proof of what I am saying."

' "A person's entitled to their thoughts," she said blandly.

' "Anonymous letters," I drawled, "you'll find come in a different category in law."

' "God works in a mysterious way 'Is wonders to perform. 'E'll see Justice is done," she said, crossing her ankles and surveying her stumpy toes.

'I took no notice. I was listening and watching the door.

' "I want to speak to you alone," I said quietly, bending my head and stroking my gloves.

'So she got down and waddled over to the door without a word, the quick-witted old monster, and appeared not in the least surprised to find Mrs Livingstone kneeling at the keyhole, for all the world as if she'd been caught at her prayers; and I'm bound to admit that she could not have looked more astounded if the god she was praying to had suddenly appeared before her.

' "Now, Fanny, it's no use looking for your letter there," said the old woman imperturbably.

' "Not a letter, Amelia," she said, scrambling to her feet. "I dropped a garnet out of Reginald's bracelet. Such a pity! I thought it might be in the mat."

' "You 'ave a good look, dear. I'll leave the door open to give you a better light," she said wickedly; but Mrs Livingstone, still mumbling apologies, had trotted away.

' "Yer can't blame poor Fanny," said Mrs Falk temperately, hitching herself back on her chair. "She wants to know how much longer she's going to have to keep me here. I dessay she don't feel it would be kind to ask me outright. I dessay she's afraid of the answer. So she listens, in case I should 'appen to mention me plans to someone else. But, poor old me, I've no plans. Where can an old woman like me go? I've no money. A few sticks of furniture and some old-fashioned gems. But what would *they* fetch? They mean more to me than they're worth, I fear . . . memories . . . memories . . . That's all I'm rich in," she said dabbing her eyes.

'I caught her eyeing me slyly behind her handkerchief, expecting me to admire her performance no doubt.

'I said sharply:

' "I'm afraid that I am only interested in establishing my father's innocence, Mrs Falk. A task which you have done your best to make impossible."

' "And all I'm interested in, Miss High-and-Mightiness, is providing a few comforts for me last days," she countered with odious familiarity.

' "Has the one anything to do with the other?" I said coldly.

'She ignored me and went on, pulling at her lower lip thoughtfully:

' "I have often wondered whether that kind-hearted young husband of yours couldn't be persuaded to do something for me."

' "You're wasting your time, Mrs Falk. Oliver hasn't a penny, as you very well know," I said firmly. I looked at the queer old thing, crazy, mumbling, repulsive, and I added clearly so that she should understand: "He couldn't find a hundred pounds to save his life."

' "Well?" she said. "You've endowed him with all yer worldly goods, ain't yer? Same thing!"

' "It comes to this, then: you expect me to keep you. You may pretend it would be Oliver, but in fact it would be me. I think, Mrs Falk, we understand one another well enough for it not to be necessary to discuss this any further," I said meaningly.

' "Just as yer please, yer ladyship!" the fantastic old creature said with a chuckle.

'I rose; I would not wait for tea, I said, and made my excuses. Having said what I had come to say there seemed to be no good reason for prolonging the interview. I was thankful to be out of the place and made off as briskly as I could. Well, I had done all that was possible, and that, I thought, was that.

'I was the more surprised then to receive a letter the very next day from her, posted in London. She must have gone back as soon as I left! She wrote in a spidery Italian hand:

' "DEAR MRS BRIDGEWATER,
      "If you are interested in Curious old papers,
I have come across some among my late
daughter's Effects which are for sale.
      "Awaiting the favour of an early reply,
            "Yours etc.,
                  "Amelia Falk."

'I hadn't a notion what the crazy old thing was talking about or why she imagined that anything of Sophia's, however "old" and "curious", could have any interest for me; but in spite of myself I sent her a wire telling her to send them immediately.

'If she was not playing some obscure game with me, I knew I could expect to receive this mysterious package of papers the following day. I thought I had locked the letter safely in my little escritoire, but by one of those kinks of the mind, I had dropped it where I sat, and late that evening Oliver found it crumpled among the cushions on the day-bed.

'Oh, my goodness, what a fuss he made about it! I could not understand it. He wanted to know why she had written to me; he got out of me when I had seen her last, and then he had to know *why* I had seen her and what I had said to her, besides. He appeared to hold me to blame for her absurd letter; or perhaps it was only that in his fright he wanted someone to scold. For he *was* frightened under all these blustering questions, I could tell. So the circumstances did

not seem propitious to tell him that I had already answered
her letter. He declared that I must have promised her
money.
' "Why, Oliver, how could I?" I protested. For he knew
perfectly well that I had nothing of my own apart from
Mama's jewellery, which had been left to me as the eldest
girl. Oliver doled out my pin-money from whatever money
it had been arranged at the time of my marriage that Papa
should allow him.
'But he grumpily maintained that I must have led her to
believe something of the sort, or why did she offer these
things for sale?
' "How should I know? The old thing's mad, I suppose."
' "My dear girl, can't you understand?" he said impatiently. "She is trying to get her hooks into you. This is
simply an attempt at blackmail."
' "But how absurd!" I cried. "What on earth does the old
creature imagine she could blackmail me about? Silly old
toad!"
' "She must think she has got some information so
prejudicial that we would be willing to pay her to suppress
it."
' "You mean, something to do with Sophia's death?" I
said.
'He shrugged.
' "I don't know," he said.
' "What ought we to do?" I asked.
' "There is only one thing to do in a case of blackmail,"
Oliver said slowly; "Inform the police."
' "Only, supposing it *was* something one would rather
people didn't know about?" I said doubtfully.
' "In that case," he said thoughtfully. "In that case, I
rather think for all our sakes, before I commit the affair into
the hands of the police, I had best find out what it is she
thinks she knows."
'He had already left for London before the mysterious
package arrived from Mrs Falk, and the "curious old

papers" were found to be letters from Oliver written to
Sophia before her marriage. From which it was evident,
even to such a pitifully ignorant little dolt as myself, that as
far back as that Sophia had been his mistress.

'They made the whole story evident. Every past detail of
the intrigue stood out with the astounding clarity of a banal
view leaping to the eye in a stereoscope. The marriage with
Papa had been an arranged affair. (*Of course you must marry
your old man, my dearest, if you can bring him up to scratch,* Oliver
had written.) I realised that for Sophia it had simply been a
method of escaping from the grinding poverty which bore
down on her so heavily. Papa's side of the bargain was that
he got *her,* that was sufficient, he must not also expect to
claim her honesty, chastity, fidelity or love.

'It seemed there had never been any question of a rupture
between the lovers; the marriage was only undertaken to
make the situation easier for them both, penniless as they
were. (*Tell him I'm your cousin,* Oliver wrote; *or make me your
brother: why not? There must be good reason to visit you frequently;
any hole-and-corner business would be decidedly too risky. Isn't there
an ugly daughter I can marry?*) I should have been amused to
see his face when she told him that there was, and that he
might certainly marry me, for if he did not, nobody else
would.

'I am not trying to make out that the letters were deliberately cynical or cruel in those passages which did not
chance to be amorous; they were simply intended to be a
cool businesslike exposition of how the practical aspects of
the plan would work out. People never recognise sin in
themselves, do they? We are always innocent in our own
eyes (except for the saints among us of course). I daresay
Sophia and Oliver considered themselves hard done by,
that life had treated them unfairly in making it "impossible" for them to marry one another when they were so
passionately in love. People seem to think they have "the
right" to love, whatever the circumstances; that the mere
strength of their desire can lift it above morality, and
absolve them from penalty.' She shrugged her plump shoul-

ders comfortably. 'Well, they paid for their pleasure, both of them,' she said, with a strain of puritanical satisfaction that sat oddly on the antique serenity of her broad brow.

'You see, my conscience gave me no rest until I took those letters to Mr Pierce. I knew he ought to see them. I knew that once he had read them and I had added to it my own knowledge, he would have quite a different view of the case. I had held back before from a sense of duty to my husband. But how much loyalty did I owe to him really? He had shown none to me. And when it came to letting my innocent father suffer for my husband's guilt, my whole soul rebelled. That was more than I could support.

'I watched the policeman reading them, his blunt forefinger following the words like a peasant. When he had finished them he put them tidily together and looked across at me, gravely.

'I said:

' "I think it is time I told you what I know."

' "I take it, ma'am, you want to make a statement," he said, and called in a constable to sit in a corner and take down my words in a notebook.

'So I began.

'Starting from the letters I traced the intrigue from its beginnings. I told him how Sophia had pretended she was going to have a baby in order to escape having to accompany my father on his travels, presumably because she could not face the prospect of being parted from Oliver for so long; and how, on the one hand, this gave her the chance of a season alone in London with her lover (an incident which Mrs Falk could corroborate) while she was supposed to be having a miscarriage; while, on the other hand, when she did later find herself genuinely with child the recent false pregnancy ruined for ever her chances of confusing the dates – as other illicitly pregnant women have done before.

'I said awkwardly:

' "The child Mrs Sheridan was bearing at the time of her death was my husband's."

'He asked as delicately as possible what proof I had.

' "That was why he killed her of course," I said simply,
and saw the policeman stiffen.

' "I have been sure of it for a long time," I told him,
"certainly ever since the day we had news of Papa's unexpectedly early return. I tell you, that sent them into a panic.
I heard them talking that same night when they thought
they were alone. It was terrifying. I had to cram my hands
into my mouth to prevent myself from crying out." I
repeated to him the conversation I heard that night, part of
which I have already told you. How in her weakness and
despair she wanted to run away with him, and he said she
must be mad to think even of wrecking all their plans and
ruining his career for good, and so on. I think now that it
was at that moment that the idea of killing her first occurred
to him; I think from the way he spoke that he was beginning
to be tired of her; I think he was afraid of her power over him
and knew he would never be free while she was alive. For
death was in his thoughts then, though it was Father's
death he spoke of.

' "If he should die," Oliver had said lightly; "that would
be one way out of the dilemma."

' "Providing he died before he had a chance to alter his
will," Sophia answered bitterly.

' "Exactly," said my husband.

'Something in his voice made her turn to look at his face.
For a long moment they stared at one another in silence,
there in the brightly gaslit room opening on to the dark
garden where I stood, the solitary audience, watching and
listening to this scene set like a play upon the stage. And it
was of a play that the abrupt terrible phrases reminded me.
It was like listening to that hideous meeting between the
Thane of Glamis and Cawdor and Lady Macbeth.

' "Why not?" Oliver answered her wordless question.

' "We dare not!" she whispered back.

' "Is there any other way?" he asked.

'They did not move nearer to one another, although their

speech was low. It was as if they were too frozen to move. They stared with glittering eyes at this vision of murder and questioned each other about it, as though it was there before them in the middle of the room.

' "How would it be done?" the woman said in a quick small voice.

' "I don't know!" he exclaimed angrily. "I don't know!"

'He had time to turn up and down the room before she said:

' "The boy keeps a deadly poison in his dark-room. It would only need a pinch."

'He said quickly, harshly:

' "It is dangerous even to utter such thoughts aloud. It was a moment of dizziness that came over me. Put it out of your mind, Sophie!"

' "Yes, Noll," she said, as meek as a wife. And with that they separated for the night. Oliver lingered for yet a moment beneath the gaselier before he reached up and pulled the chain and the light expired with a faint blue hiss.

'Mr Pierce rather peevishly asked why I had not immediately come to them with this information and so made it possible to prevent the crime. By not doing so I had made myself into an accessory before the fact, a serious offence.

'I stammered out that I had not known I was doing wrong. I had not thought it conceivable to complain to the police about a crime that had not yet been committed. If such an idea had entered my head, I would only have supposed they would laugh at me. Besides, I did not really believe it myself. If I was horrified by their words it was not because I believed them capable of putting them into action, but because the words themselves revealed such baseness, such depths of unimagined hatred in their cruel minds. And was it a thing any nice-minded young woman could bring herself to mention to strangers? Was it a thing one could bear to tell about one's own family, one's own husband? It meant revealing too much, too much. Besides, what proof had I that this conversation had ever truly taken place?'

The angular young person in the corner made a movement of protest, but Miss Hine did not permit an interruption at this point; she swept on:

'Afterwards was a different matter. For one thing it had become a practical issue, a question of justice. For another, the proof of my assertion was that I now knew how the crime had been committed.

'Oliver had substituted the poison for one of Sophia's digestive-powders. (You remember she suffered from indigestion, and the paper that contained the last powder she took had been found by her body.) He had only to tip out the digestive-powder and tip in its place an equal quantity of poison, fold the paper over it in its original folds and then replace it among the others in the box. Since she took three or four powders a day, it was not impossible to calculate when she should take the fatal dose, and arrange for himself to be absent when it occurred. As he did.

'I can see you are wondering how I came to know about it. You see, Oliver must have made the substitution in Harry's dark-room, and he could hardly just throw the harmless powder on the floor or anywhere where it might attract someone's notice later. So he tipped it into a corner of his handkerchief, intending, I suppose, to throw it away when he got outside. But he had first to get the poison back into the box in the drawer in Sophia's room unobserved. And in the tension of this he simply forgot about the other. I found the handkerchief rolled up in his pocket when I was getting his things together to be washed. I put it on one side, meaning to ask him what it was; but then Sophia was killed and it drove all such trivialities out of my mind. I didn't remember it again until the inquest. When I came home after that, I tasted it on the tip of my finger and realised that it was the same stuff as the powders Sophia took. And then I did begin to wonder, I admit.

'I didn't say anything to Oliver about it, after all. But I kept the powder carefully in the secret drawer of my jewel-case, until I handed it over to Mr Pierce when I had concluded my statement. And after that there was nothing more for me to do,' said Miss Hine a trifle smugly.

'And what did Mr Pierce say, I wonder?' observed Mr Jones drily. 'Was he pleased with the way you had tied up his case for him and fastened it with blue ribbons?'

'Dear me, I don't see that he had anything to complain about, had he? After all,' she said archly, 'he had said I ought to have been in the Force the first time he saw me. Besides, he had still to find out whether my statement was true, and more – he had to prove it. He had to find witnesses he could bring into Court, for as Oliver's wife I could not give evidence against him in this matter. I had made my declared statement to the police and that was all I might do; it was up to them to find the necessary evidence to support it.'

'And did he?' asked Mr Jones.

'Find the evidence for the Prosecution?' said Miss Hine. 'Oh, yes.'

CHAPTER THIRTEEN

THE END OF THE STORY

Miss Hine rose at this point and looked out of the window to where the sun, a fiery ball flung out of the sky by a Great Magician, appeared to be magically arrested in its stupendous rush towards them and to hang poised for a timeless moment a foot above the horizon. She leaned out, cupping her mouth in her hands like a muezzin, and called below. A faint cry answered her.

'What is it?' asked the young man nervously.

She turned to smile at him.

'Come!' she said. 'It is nearly time for you to leave and you must have something to eat before you go.'

'I couldn't eat a thing,' said Mr Jones positively. 'I'd much rather hear the rest of your story.'

Miss Hine as positively insisted that he must eat. She would continue her tale at the table. She warned him that in the East it was as unthinkable to refuse to accept hospitality as it was to refuse to give it. Was he afraid of being served with sheep's eyes? Had she not promised him a simple repast with no esoteric delicacies to upset his soul or his digestion? Besides, he must learn to practise stoicism: what would he do if at Mahmoud Kahn's he was expected to eat fried snake with mangoes for breakfast?

Mr Jones, trying not to heave at the mere idea, replied, *'Autre pays, autre moeurs'* and remembered the great thing was to remain cool and detached in all circumstances. A precept he attempted to put into practice as he followed the old woman into the courtyard.

Mr Jones's supper was spread on a marble table beneath the jasmine. The little fountain splashed its precise pattern unendingly into the air. On a dish of green leaves stood a round white mound of sheep's cheese adorned with jetty fragments of pickled walnuts. There were bowls of curd, and candied citrons, and a salad of rose petals garnished with olives and green pimentos, and bread with poppy seeds on it.

Miss Hine resumed her narrative.

'All this while Papa was sunk into a melancholic lethargy from which it seemed nothing could rouse him. He sat all day with his head in his hands and would not trouble to answer when he was spoken to. Naturally I was worried about him; unhappy at his unhappiness. I hoped that when he learned about Oliver's treachery he would turn to me again and I would win back his love.

'But when I went to him, where he sat perpetually by the open window, not watching the empty sea but staring between his hands at the carpet, and knelt by his side to tell him, all he at last brought out rustily was: "Does it matter?"

'I put my arms about him.

' "We only have each other now," I said. "We were neither of us loved for ourselves, you see, dearest."

' "Does it matter?" Papa repeated dully.

' "But, dearest, don't you see? Now we can prove your innocence to the world," I said eagerly.

' "Does it matter?" Papa said.

'My poor Papa! His mind had quite gone. I had him to myself all right, he was as much mine as ever I could wish; like a baby, a great melancholy baby – wasn't there a song called "Melancholy Baby" years ago? – well, that was Papa till he died. Happily, he did not live long. The rain blew in on him one day as he sat at his open window and he caught cold, and died because he had no will to live.'

She paused to strip a fig carefully of its shiny purple skin.

'But your husband?' said Mr Jones, mashing sheep cheese on to a seeded crust. 'What happened to him?'

'Oliver? He was brought to trial at the last Assize of the year before the Christmas recess. Poor unfortunate fellow,' she said calmly, 'he did not stand a chance. The jury was only away twenty minutes. Of course you must remember this was before the Criminal Evidence Act of 1898 and so he could not be examined by the Defence to give evidence in his own favour, which I daresay made it very hard for him – and very easy for the Prosecution. However, I comfort myself with the thought that it would not have made any difference in the end. Justice must be satisfied.'

'Well, *really* – ' said Mr Jones in a strangled voice, as if he had just found a sheep's eye or a morsel of fried snake in his mouth and did not know what to do with it.

'Of course I knew nothing of all this at the time,' Miss Hine said reprovingly. 'I was desperately ill for weeks with brain-fever. That was when they cut off all my heavy brown hair.' She stroked her poll meditatively. 'And it was so cool and agreeable that I've worn it like this ever since.'

'But your husband?' Mr Jones insisted.

The old woman sighed portentously.

'The horror of that time is something I can still hardly bear to discuss. You see, the child was born – dead, on the day its father was hanged in the prison precincts . . . It was a long while before I was strong enough to travel, but as soon as I could, I left England for ever and changed my name, so that the unhappy past would no longer pursue me. I had lost everything and must start life all over again. And I'm bound to say that I think I've done pretty well, considering,' she added complacently.

Mr Jones stared at her in horror. He thrust the pretty pink salad away from him, as though the sight of it made him ill.

'Do you mean to tell me that you deliberately allowed your husband to hang?' he said incredulously.

'Allowed?' repeated the old woman with wide blue eyes as innocent as flowers. 'I don't know what you mean? What could I have done?'

'You could have prevented it,' he said in a low tense voice.

'Even if I could – which I don't for an instant admit – why on earth should I want to prevent him from getting his just deserts? He'd never been a particularly good husband, I think you'll admit. And you surely cannot imagine I loved him.'

'What has love to do with it?' said Mr Jones outraged. 'It was simply Justice.'

'That's what I say. It was Justice,' agreed the old woman placidly. 'But you surely haven't finished your meal? There's plenty of time yet. Come, you must try one of my specialities, a peach dusted with ground almonds and cinnamon.' She called out a complicated order to a woman in the heavy black hood Mahommedan women wear before strange men and she slipped away into the shadows.

'I cannot imagine your purpose in telling me this abominable story if you did not want me to discover the truth?' Mr Jones said severely.

'The truth?' she echoed, surprised, as though she had never heard the word before. 'What is the truth, pray?'

Confused by the barbaric heated impressions of the afternoon and the coolly remote story from the distant past, for a vain lost minute it was hard to find reality.

With an effort, Mr Jones said:

'The truth is that *you murdered Sophia* yourself.'

The old woman stared at him in frosty amazement. He could hear his heart beating in the silence. It was perhaps unforgivable to insult one's hostess? He waited in alarm.

At oast she uttered, coolly, ironically:

'May one venture to enquire how you arrived at that remarkable deduction?'

'You were the one who had most reason to want her out of the way,' said Mr Jones sulkily. 'You were insanely jealous of her influence over your father because – let's face it – you were in love with him yourself. However much you tried you couldn't conceal that you hated her.'

'I haven't tried for a moment to conceal that I hated her;

she was a very wicked character; but that doesn't mean I killed her, you know. If one killed everybody one hated, one's relations would hardly be safe, poor things,' she said drily. 'But, go on, tell me how you think I did it.'

'You were the only one who knew how Sophia was killed. Doesn't that strike you as odd?'

'I think, my dear young sir, that you are being wise after the event,' she said good-humouredly. 'You might remember that I was an exceptionally sheltered girl of only nineteen. You might say, a child. How should I know of such things?'

'The cyanide was there under your hand and *you* knew it was a deadly poison. You were just as able as your husband was to change the powder in one of Sophia's digestive doses, and we know that you had a much stronger motive than he had.'

'Possibly. But it happened to be found in *his* handkerchief, not mine,' she pointed out, unmoved.

'I maintain that you fudged that evidence against him. All that stuff about finding the powder in a corner of his handkerchief! You put it there yourself of course. I thought it was odd the way you twisted your report of the conversation you overheard between Oliver and Sophia when you told it to the police. It hardly corresponded with the version you told me first: then it was *he* who suggested running away and *she* who said it would only lead to scandal and ruin. Was it then that you decided to kill her, I wonder?'

'Murder my stepmother and make my own husband the scapegoat, how could such a dreadful idea have even entered my mind?'

'I'm not suggesting you meant your husband to hang then. I think you hoped it would be considered suicide. I don't think you realised all the enquiry that would follow her death. You became more and more rattled as one after another of the family were involved in the scandal, though I don't really believe you cared twopence what happened to any of them except your father. That was your obsession.

And when it came to the point where he was actually in real danger as the likeliest suspect, then you had to act, and act quickly, if he was to be saved. As you admitted yourself, you would almost have given yourself up to save him. But instead you found a scapegoat to be the "real culprit". When you went to see Mrs Falk that day at her sister's house, I don't believe for an instant that it was with any idea of "stopping her mouth" as you pretended, for by that time the damage was done and the exhumation ordered, so there was no longer any purpose in threatening her. No, you went there to see if she could be bribed to give you evidence of some sort against your husband. Oh, I'm not saying you asked for it bluntly like that,' he said quickly as she started to protest. 'But without putting it into words you managed to make it quite clear to her what you meant, with the way you stressed that Oliver couldn't find a hundred pounds to *save his life*, and that Mrs Falk evidently expected you to keep her for the rest of her life, and so on. Meaning that if she played her part properly and produced the necessary evidence she could rely on you for the money.'

'This is sheer invention,' she said, but her eyes watched him sharply.

'Oh, I grant you pretended not to know what she was writing about when she offered the "Curious old papers" for sale, but you were careful to send for the papers before letting Oliver know about them, and then you sent him off on a wild goose errand to fetch them when you knew they were no longer there, because you wanted him safely out of the way when you presented your evidence to the police. Did the old lady realise, I wonder, that you were buying the letters not to protect but to *betray* your husband? Or did you trick her too?'

'Mrs Falk wanted her revenge just as much as I did. You might just as well say that she used me to do her dirty and dangerous work for her.'

'So you admit it!' said Mr Jones in a shocked voice. 'To protect your father, you had your husband killed! You deliberately allowed an innocent man to hang!'

'In the circumstances, I should hardly have thought "allowed" was the *mot juste*,' Miss Hine said mildly. 'I should have said "arranged" was nearer the mark.'

'But you are really horrible, wicked,' muttered Mr Jones fearfully.

'Oh, you mustn't think me a monster. I was only a friendless unhappy girl trying to do what was best for all concerned. You cannot deny that Sophia was a thoroughly evil and dissolute woman who would only have brought shame and disgrace on us all if she had been let live. I can't find it in my heart to blame myself for what I did then. Do try and feel some sympathy for that poor bewildered girl,' Miss Hine said in reasonable tones, which yet only succeeded in affronting Mr Jones's moral sense the more.

'Sympathy for you!' said Mr Jones severely. 'Why, you have no more conscience than a cat! You betrayed everybody without the least sign of feeling, without a hint of remorse or guilt.'

'It was they who were to blame; they were all so wicked,' she said blandly. 'They corrupted my innocence.'

'If you were innocent, God help the guilty!' exclaimed Mr Jones piously.

'Well, really!' said Miss Hine with a jocund laugh. 'There's nothing like insulting one's hostess. Oh, bless you, I don't mind! I've thoroughly enjoyed telling you about it and you've been a very patient listener. And an exceptionally clever one too, I'm sure not one person in a hundred would have guessed. I hope you haven't been bored.'

But Mr Jones was not to be won by flattery – from a murderess.

'Not bored,' he said sharply, spooning up the last of the peach juices with its haunting almond fragrance, 'but very decidedly appalled.'

'Oh, my dear young man, aren't you taking it all rather too seriously? We don't want to be priggish, do we? After all, it happened a great while ago and it would be foolish to pretend that it mattered to anybody now. There are far too many people in the world anyway, and most of them unnecessary. Of course I felt a little uncomfortable at the time, I admit, but one can't brood for ever and it's wonderful how quickly unpleasant memories do fade from the mind. I think I may say I've had a very happy and successful life, on the whole,' she concluded complacently.

'You're inhuman! I thought at least that unpunished murderers were haunted by their own consciousness of guilt,' Mr Jones said angrily.

'It's a funny thing,' said Miss Hine, 'I've always noticed that it is the people who have never done anything wrong in this world who are tortured with feelings of guilt. It does seem unfair. While I thrive. Not a twinge of remorse to trouble my sleep or disturb my digestion.' She chuckled pleasantly. 'Perhaps we should all be more confident and healthy-minded if we had a murder or two behind us.'

But Mr Jones was extremely unamused. That the guilty should be happy and the blameless suffer gave him a feeling of vertigo, as though the ground was being cut away from under his feet. Where now was the attitude of philosophical detachment on which he prided himself?

'You understand that I shall have to report this as soon as I return to England,' he said stiffly.

'I shouldn't bother,' said Miss Hine calmly. 'You will only bring ridicule and contempt upon yourself, raking over the dead old rubbish of half a century ago.'

'I assure you, it's useless – ' began Mr Jones, but Miss Hine cut him short by saying that if he wished to take-off before sundown it was time for him to leave.

The etiquette of taking leave of one's hostess gracefully when she is a self-confessed murderess is uncertain. Mr Jones felt awkward. He tried to be austere, but she was so undefeatably amiable that she·made him feel a fool, and a gauche young fool at that. His threat to inform against her left her curiously unperturbed. Didn't she take him seriously then? Or had she some reason for not considering him dangerous? What reason could she have, a murderess? *A murderess!* What one has done once, one may do again, he realised, feeling the weakness of fear in all his joints. How insanely trusting he had been! As though she would have dared confess all that unless she had made it quite safe for herself . . . *Something in his food.* She had been so damnably insistent that he should take supper. But then she hadn't known he had guessed her secret? He recollected, with a lurch of terror, her calling suddenly for the peaches and ground almonds . . . ground almonds! . . . the taste came back into his mouth, haunting, pungent . . .

From a long way away he heard the old woman saying, 'Now, don't forget to write and let me know you've arrived. I shall be so interested to learn what becomes of you. You should go a long way. *Such* a clever young man!'

She might have been a fond aunt saying good-bye to a favourite nephew if it had not been for the irony of her tone.

The gate clanged shut behind him. He was alone beneath the great hollow sky. In the afterglow the village looked like blocks of pink ice-cream. The airplane was a small black cross in the distance. He wondered how long the poison would take to work. The cold wind that blew off the desert at sunset made him shiver with a sudden fever. He began to hurry over the rough ground. He wanted to get to Ras Ali before he died . . . to tell him . . . His temples were throbbing louder and louder . . . till he realised the throbbing was not in his head but in the waiting aircraft . . . He stumbled on.

Ras Ali saluted, once again competent, cheery, intrepid.

'Ras Ali, I'm ill,' gasped Mr Jones. And was. Exceedingly.

The relief of having got the poison out of his system was enormous. He climbed into the rickety little machine almost jauntily, he was surprised to find it felt quite like home to him. The plane shook all over and raced forward bumpily.

'Good-bye, Madam Borgia!' said Mr Jones aloud with sardonic triumph.

And presently, from the ground, only its steady track distinguished the plane's crimson tail-light from the fireflies darting boldly through the gathering dusk.

EPILOGUE OR COD-PIECE

Lancelot Jones did arrive safely at Bandrapore, the little Indian State governed by Mahmoud Kahn, and found it all very quaint and agreeable. Mahmoud Kahn's palace was fantastically gorgeous and incredibly primitive. The Court Officials looked as if they were dressed for close-ups in a Cecil B. de Mille epic of the East, with jewelled turbans and glittering orders on their brocaded coats, and bare feet and legs. On the other hand, although Mr Jones turned over his food suspiciously, to his relief he was given kedgeree for breakfast and not fried snakes.

If one cannot take out one's impressions and air them in conversation, the next best thing is to write a letter to describe what one thinks and feels and observes. There was no one for Mr Jones to talk to, so he devoted one morning to writing a really amusing account (deft and witty) of his experiences to an Oxford friend.

He described the elephant-porch on the palace, of fretted pink marble forty feet high; he described a bird that perched on his balcony and whistled to him maddeningly in the moonlight; he described his eight-year-old charge, a fierce little huntsman, delicate as a Persian miniature, undisciplined, courteous, weeping with love for a Ranee in a neighbouring State, to whom he wrote overwrought and yearning love-poems; and he described his journey over in the rickety little plane and touched airily on his adventure mid-way.

'Came down in the desert, apparently miles from any human habitation. But luckily found a minute village with one decent house in it, wherein I encountered a curious old character who called herself Alva Hine, but whose name was really Blanche Sheridan. A *very* odd story there! I wonder if you have ever come across the name in your pursuit of paper-criminology? If you have, I'll tell you more; *not at all* what you would expect from your readings.'

In the course of time his friend answered him, and halfway down the second page wrote:

'Of course I've heard of Alva Hine, my dear chap. Who hasn't? Fancy running into her in that god-forsaken spot! How really *odd*! It must have been a most entertaining experience for you. I wish you had told me more about her. It is really rather maddening of you! Do be sure and tell me more when next you write.'

But by that time the experience had already become the *past* and it would have been a colossal bore to have to write about it. He never answered the letter. Instead he had become deeply absorbed in the pleasures of pig-sticking – he, who had always so despised hunting for its futility and meaningless savagery! Oh, he could have written a poem himself (for it was beginning to dawn on him now what poetry was for) on the exultation of riding into the fresh delicious morning, so full of well-being that it made him bellow like an opera-singer with delight.

He never troubled to write to Miss Hine, though for the first week he did think out one or two crisp letters, but it was too much bother to put them down on paper, and besides, he was no longer so sure she had tried to kill him, it might have been only the upsetting combination of excitement, excessive heat, and rich exotic food. He had no wish to make a fool of himself. He put it out of his mind.

At last he returned to England (having had a wonderful time, though he had utterly failed to screw an anna of salary out of the Kahn, who only appeared twice during the whole of his stay), to settle dimly into rather a dreary job in a rather dreary tutorial establishment, and life became very dull. Something seemed missing, that he did not know by the name of Romance. He seriously considered joining that great sect who write books about their experiences; he fancied he might write a book about India in his spare time – something very simple and natural like Hindoo Holiday!

And when he did go to the police they were simply no use at all. It was preposterous! They said they had no record of the Sheridan case. They weren't even interested in his account of it. They seemed to think he was a crank or potty. Mr Jones was most annoyed. He became something of a bore on the subject.

In December, just before Christmas, he received a parcel forwarded from his College; the precise agreeable shape of a book. He noticed it had not come from the Oxford booksellers, but from a firm of publishers. Something he had ordered and forgotten about perhaps? Or an early Christmas present?

It was neither, strictly speaking. Or perhaps it was both.

Across its bold violet jacket was printed in crimson NO MOURNERS BY REQUEST! and scrawled under that, a huge white signature: *ALVA HINE.*

Mr Jones stared stupefied at this, and at the words underneath 'Alva Hine's 100th Crime Novel'! He was unable to make sense of anything – even the title. He turned the first pages gingerly, as if they might be contagious or contain some horrible surprise. The name Blanche Rose caught his eye, and here and there a phrase that seemed oddly familiar. And then he saw it!

Between the Title Page and the Table of Contents, printed alone on the page in bold black type he saw:

> 'Dedicated without his permission
> to the Patient Listener
> who had
> An Afternoon to Kill.'

And after a dizzying moment of bewilderment, Mr Jones began to laugh.